blue
rider
press

SEVEN
DEADLIES

SEVEN DEADLIES

▸ A CAUTIONARY TALE ◂

Gigi Levangie

Illustrations by Cecilia Ruiz

BLUE RIDER PRESS

a member of Penguin Group (USA)

New York

Fic
Levange

10/ /13
Iy
25⁹⁵

blue
rider
press

Published by the Penguin Group
Penguin Group (USA) LLC
375 Hudson Street
New York, New York 10014, USA

USA · Canada · UK · Ireland · Australia
New Zealand · India · South Africa · China

penguin.com
A Penguin Random House Company

Library of Congress Cataloging-in-Publication Data

Grazer, Gigi Levangie.
Seven deadlies : a cautionary tale / Gigi Levangie ;
illustrations by Cecilia Ruiz.
p.   cm
ISBN 978-0-399-16673-0
1. Deadly sins—Fiction.   2. Beverly Hills (Calif.)—Fiction.
3. Humorous fiction.   I. Ruiz, Cecilia, illustrator.   II. Title.
PS3557.R2913S48   2013   2013029104
813'.54—dc23

Printed in the United States of America
1   3   5   7   9   10   8   6   4   2

BOOK DESIGN BY MEIGHAN CAVANAUGH

To Thug the Elder

and Thug the Younger,

otherwise known as

Thomas and Patrick

Dear Bennington Admissions Committee:

What you are about to read is exactly how it happened. I fancy myself a wordsmith—a browner, female Bret Easton Ellis (one of your esteemed alumni), if you will—but what I have attached here as my future admissions essay is strictly journalistic. I am reporting the stories exactly how I witnessed them.

Thank you for your kind consideration. I look forward to your response.

Miss Perry Gonzales
Mark Frost Academy, Class of 20—

A Brief Monologue to Answer Your Questions:
Okay, I should introduce myself properly, right? That's what my mother says. Yelena Maria Gonzales, R.N. I hear her voice inside my head only constantly. My mom's a nurse, one of nine children, born in the Yucatán, in the southeastern corner of Mexico, in the year 1972.

My name is Perry. Perry Gonzales, no middle name. I'm fourteen years old. I'm a freshman at Mark Frost Academy (sponsored by Wild Pockets Banking, Ltd.). Do I have to mention that I'm a scholarship student? Figure it out—I'm the daughter of a single mother, I'm full-blooded Chicana, in the heat of a Valley August my skin is dark as coffee grounds, and somehow my face shows up on the school website every year.

Look it up. There I am. That's me, in my uniform, playing clarinet, with my black Indian hair in braids, oh, and the braces—it's an old picture.

Don't I look happy?

My mom and I, we live alone in a one-bedroom apartment in North Hollywood. No brothers and no sisters. My dad is long gone. I catch the bus every morning to go up to the top of Beverly Vista, where Mark Frost Academy sits at the end of a long drive. The first thing you see in front of my school is a huge, Italianate fountain, donated by the Spielberg family.

You can see what I'm dealing with here.

I have my own money, though. I've been babysitting since I was eight years old. There's a ton of kids in my apartment building. The moms all work in the city—they clean houses, mostly. Sometimes there's more than one family living in an apartment. I've saved my dollars up. I want some spending money when I get to Bennington.

I'm going to be a writer. Apparently all you do at Bennington is write. And write some more. And the students talk about writing and take it seriously. And all of this takes place in peace and quiet.

Away. Away. Far away.

I've been writing things down since before I could talk. No, it's true—I didn't say a word until I was five, in kindergarten. That word was *abogado*. Lawyer. It's what they have on the back of every RTD bus in Los Angeles. *Abogado*. The teachers had thought I was retarded, just another little brown-skinned issue to deal with. My mother knew different—she never pushed me to talk, as she never pushes me now. She just . . . listens.

And when she finally does speak, you'd better listen back. Her words are economic, but they carry great weight.

In the silence of our lives, I learned two things early on: I learned to read, and I learned to observe.

Our apartment is white stucco with a few sliding glass windows; it looks like a box on sticks. Every week, graffiti appears on the side facing the alleyway—and every week the Korean owner comes and paints it over. So in certain patches, there are twenty layers of paint. It looks like a white on white quilt.

Someone named "Clownie" must have been shot and killed over the weekend, because today *RIP Clownie* is being painted over.

My mom and I could move. She makes pretty good money. But she and I, we're savers. Plus, she sends a lot of her salary home, to the Yucatán, to her family. Besides, we've grown used to it—we know our neighbors, we've watched the little ones grow. They're *familia*. Whenever we think about moving, we ask ourselves—where?

Where is better than here, for us? For now?

So, I'm not one to brag, but I'm pretty much the smartest girl in my class. There are about sixty kids per class, from seventh to twelfth grade. My grades are excellent. My motivation is high. I don't drink or do drugs or hang out with the bad kids. I'm pretty much all business. My life is not going to end here, in this part of Los Angeles, or even at Bennington.

I'm going places.

Which brings me to my latest business venture. Baby-sitting teenagers.

A few of the moms at school talk to my mother. You should see them. They gather around her like fans. She's barely five feet tall in her nurse's shoes. Her thick black braid circles her shoulders. She is beautiful and regal, a Latina queen. And she never, ever wears makeup, not even lip gloss.

They want to know the secret. *Why is your daughter such a good girl? How is Perry so smart?*

And . . . *Where did we go wrong?*

Their diamond tennis bracelets shimmer with every gesture. I look at those bracelets and want to eat them.

Where did we go wrong?

Can Perry help out this weekend? I have to go to New York for Fashion Week. Can Perry help out Thursday night? I have to go to a premiere. Can Perry come over after school? My daughter needs help with biology . . . and staying out of my medicine cabinet.

I get paid $40 an hour. I have business cards.

I cannot be corrupted.

I will not be corrupted.

I am just taking notes.

I swear.

Welcome.

My name is Perry Gonzales. I am a ninth-grade student at Mark Frost Academy. The stories you are about to read are true. The names have been changed to protect the not-so-innocent.

LUST

Dear Admissions Committee:

Hi.

In my opinion, there are three types of ignorance:

Deliberate (conspiracy theorists, Ron Paul, KKK Grand Wizards)

Stupid but Teachable (children and grandchildren of KKK Grand Wizards)

Just Don't Know Any Better (Real Housewives of Anywhere, 98 percent of celebrities)

The Blogsnot family (pronounced "BLOG-snoot") falls somewhere between Deliberate and Just Doesn't Know Any Better. They do not appear to be Stupid but Teachable. There's no evidence of their being teachable.

This story will serve as an example.

As you know, my mother, the estimable Yelena Maria Gonzales, is a registered nurse. In other words, Mama ain't no dummy. She is the four-foot-ten distillation of the Mayan culture; her people created chocolate and the number zero—imagine a world without chocolate or zero. Let's give the Mayans some props.

So I noticed the dreaded Mark Frost Academy parent potluck dinner looming on the school calendar. Potluck dinners don't happen at my old public school. Trust me.

I made it clear to my mother that she didn't have to go, certainly not on my behalf.

My mother insisted on going. She would change shifts to be on time. She made her famous (in our apartment building, anyway) chimichangas in a Pyrex dish that outweighed her and packed it in the trunk of her car.

I was nervous. My mother is strong and confident, but even Beyoncé would feel insecure next to the Mark Frost parents. And to be honest, in the weeks that I'd been a student, I'd kept a lot from my mother. For the first time, I didn't tell her everything that happened in my day. I didn't, for example, tell her about what I learned outside of class: the difference between a Bentley and a Tesla, a Birkin and a Chanel—things I knew nothing about when I started.

Things I wish I didn't know now.

I didn't tell her about the sideways glances and the snickers. About the girl who asked me if I cleaned toilets during recess.

About the boy who asked me if I spoke English.

I didn't want to burden her.

Let's put it this way, Admissions Committee: These Mark Frosties just weren't our peeps.

I did homework at our kitchen table and pictured Mama driving the ten-year-old Toyota Camry she was so proud of, with its seat heater and pop-up coffee cup holder, chugging up the hill to Blogsnot Manor.

I could see her squaring her shoulders and arguing with the valet over taking her car keys. "Where exactly do you want to take my car?" she would demand. She would inform them that she could park her own car, thank you.

I love her so much, you have to understand. She's all I have.

And she's more than enough.

I watched the clock, finished up homework, heated up leftovers, chased the neighbor kids who played tag in the hallway, watched *American Idol*, and prayed that Mom would survive her first American potluck.

I had fallen asleep on the couch when I was awakened by light footsteps coming up the stairs. The screen door creaked open. Keys jangled.

"Mama?" I jumped up.

Yelena Maria Gonzales smiled when she saw my expression.

"*Mija,*" she said, "why are you worried? Those people are so funny."

"Why, Mama?"

"I can't tell you how many parents asked me to take their coats," she said, giggling.

My heart sank. I knew it.

"Oh, *mija*. No worries," she said, grabbing me by the shoulders. "Soon, they will all be working for you. I know this like I know my own heart."

She put her feet up, and I took off her shoes and rubbed her tiny feet. They were often sore from standing all day long. She closed her eyes.

"*Mija*, you want to be a writer," she said, opening her dark eyes and staring at me.

"Yes, Mama."

"Keep your ears and eyes open. With these people, you will find many stories. More stories than any of us have years."

She closed her eyes again and started to nod off. Then she startled and fished a card out of her sweater pocket.

"Call this woman. This Blogsnot woman. *Su hija*, she needs help," Yelena Maria Gonzales said. "*Oye*, does she need help."

Sometimes, strange things happen in the strangest of places, and sometimes, strange things happen in the most normal of places.

This is one of those not-so-normal-places stories.

About a not-so-normal family. The Blogsnots.

But first, a word to clarify:

Dear Admissions Committee: The word *lust* as used here, in this not-so-normal story, is not about lust as experienced by, say, Angelina Jolie for Brad Pitt, or Brad Pitt for his reflection. There will be no bodily contact at all in this story, and certainly no kissing or, as Patricio, a five-year-old boy who lives in my building, says, "making up."

Meet Porscha Crisp Blogsnot, the apple of her parents' eye. She was cute as a shorter-than-average button and absolutely charming, with her hot-pink lynx-collared coats and her hot-pink dyed-to-match Lhasa apso(s) and her hot-pink diamond stud belly-button ring she got to match Mommy's.

Tiny, tubby Irving Blogsnot and his tiny, tubby wife,

Shelley Blogsnot, lived with Porscha and her younger, almost-normal-sized (thanks to the growth shots) brother, L.V., in a marble mansion in a gated land known as Beverly Vista, where celebrities and coyotes roam.

Every morning, a limo picked up young Porscha and deposited her two blocks away at my school, Mark Frost Academy (sponsored by Wild Pockets Banking, Ltd.). As I've learned, having been lucky enough to spend time with the Blogsnots ("lucky" being a relative term), Porscha couldn't possibly walk for two reasons. 1. Rich people live in places where sidewalks don't exist, and 2. It's very difficult to walk on five-inch heels (as any full-grown person of the female persuasion will tell you. Or your uncle whose favorite holiday is Halloween).

A typical, tiring week for Porscha went something like this:

Monday: Got up late. Ate caviar and blinis in bed. Remembered that it was a school day. Got dressed, matchy-matchy with Mommy. Was taken to school by her driver. Gave teacher a note saying she was too weak to play soccer. Again. Left school during Spanish period for a trunk show at Dolce & Gabbana (it's Italian).

Later, I came in to tutor her in math, Spanish, and everything else as she did a fashion show for me in her room. She couldn't believe I'd never read *Vogue* magazine. She was afraid I might be "special."

Tuesday: Repeated all of the above, but left school during Computer Studies for eyebrow waxing with Mommy at Anastasia Salon.

I came in to tutor Porscha as she lay in bed, tired from the eyebrow waxing. I read to her from her science textbook. Shelley Blogsnot came in after firing the staff—again!—to ask me if my mom was available to clean the house.

"My mother's a registered nurse," I would tell her, suppressing an urge to choke someone.

"Does she do windows?" Shelley would ask.

Wednesday: Repeated all of the above (including Shelley Blogsnot firing more staff), but left school early to fly to Idaho on a G5 (a very fast private jet) to pick up a new Lhasa apso (a tiny, not very fast dog).

I turned down chances to tutor on jet rides. Private jets make me nervous. They are small, and I fear that

SEVEN DEADLIES

God doesn't like rich people and I could get caught up by mistake. Death by association, as it were.

Thursday: Stayed home from school, too weak to get out of bed because of the plane trip yesterday. Mommy set up in-home manicure/pedicure and seaweed facial. New Lhasa apso got run over in the driveway by Mr. Blogsnot, who drove his bright yellow Ferrari like a rocket.

"Oopsies!" Porscha said when she heard the news.

I came in to tutor, but the Blogsnots needed to meet with the animal communicator to "talk" to Porscha's newly expired Lhasa apso. Or is it Llasa Appso? (One day, I will remember the correct spelling of *Lhasa apso*. In my defense, it is not an SAT word.)

Friday: Went to school late and left early. Had a very special Mommy and Me day at the Rodeo Collection (where they ate sushi and picked out matching tennis bracelets at Tiffany). Made plans to pick up a new puppy in Utah next week.

Porscha, who was skinny-skinny and had crooked teeth (she cut off her braces with diamond-encrusted nail clippers), had all the friends money could buy. She had all the teeny, tiny dogs that money could buy, too. But she was always losing her dogs—they got hit by cars or eaten by coyotes. Did she care?

Porscha refused to acknowledge her little brother, L.V. (named after Mommy's favorite luggage), because she still hadn't forgiven Daddy and Mommy (or, as she called them, Irving and Shell, or Stupid One and Stupid Two . . . or worse) for having another baby after they'd already had her.

All of her worries, cares, and incidentals (like disappearing pets) were secondary, however, because all Porscha really cared about in the world was one thing: the Judas Brothers.

Just who are these Judas Brothers?

Look, I like the Judas Brothers—they're cute and bouncy and appear bereft of genitalia. (I'm sorry to use the word *genitalia*, but my mother said I must be honest if I am going to be a writer.) However, I'm not obsessed with the Judas Brothers. They're adorable and all, but they're not paying my rent, got it?

Here is Porscha's latest entry from her blog:

SEVEN DEADLIES

Porscha Crisp Blogsnot

Okay, wow, like, u know, the Judas Brothers are so friggin' HOT! I mean, yeah, they are, like, CRAZY HOT! I love them sosososososo much! I mean, I would totally, like, give up everything for just one JB! I mean, I would give up my family if Aspen Judas would just, like, look at me. They are so beeyond talented! They are the best singers like ever in the whole world! They are, like, one million hundred trillion times better than, like, Justin Mayer or John Timberlake or whatever. And did I say they are the cutest ever, because they are sooooooooo super cutie! When I think about the Judas Brothers, I feal sick. Like I'm going to throw up. That's why I can't go to school so much, because I feel sick when I think of them and I can't concentrayt, so I have Perry tuetor me at home now, which is, like, AWESUM. But then I feel sick at home, so Shell takes me out to lunch or shopping. Shopping makes me feel better, so I'm not dizzy. But then when I shop I think about shopping for something the JBs would like. And when I eat, I only eat food that I know the JBs like. Like chicken wings, which are so totally gross and dizgusting, sometimes they have tiny chicken hares, but I eat, like, twenty a day! Also, I learned how to read from *Preteen Scream Magazine* (online edition), and I read all about how the JBs grew up and their likes and dislikes—they don't like girls who are mean! That's so friggin' cool! So, like, I'm trying to be nicer and stuff, but it's hard when you're so much better than other peeple!

Do you see what I had to deal with here?

Porscha Crisp Blogsnot's fourteenth birthday was one month away (yes, I know, her emotional maturity stopped at eight and a half). Little Porscha had one wish this birthday, the same as her last three: She wanted Daddy to kidnap a Judas Brother. She wasn't picky— she'd take any of them.

There's Aspen Judas (he's the cutest), Lukas Judas (he's the oldest), and Jo Jo Judas (he's the baby).

The Judas Brothers were born and raised in the hills

of Kentucky by their hardworking preschool teacher/ church choir singer mom and beet farmer dad. Despite their fame (according to *Preteen Scream Magazine* [online edition]), they are good boys with good grooming habits, and when they are home in Kentucky, they dig up beets twelve hours a day.

Anyway, Daddy Blogsnot (Irving, to you and me) told Porscha that he could not and would not kidnap a Judas Brother. He tried it once, several years ago, and almost lost a thumb. "It's just not as easy as all that, honey," he told Porscha. "They have huge bodyguards!"

(Note to Admissions Committee: I, Perry Gonzales, am not much of an artist, but I will include a drawing of the Judas Brothers' Samoan bodyguards.)

Shelley Blogsnot told me she wouldn't talk to Irving for a whole week because he broke Porscha's little heart; he let a few burly bodyguards, who carry sharp objects and are black belts in tae kwon do, stand in the way of their daughter's happiness!

Porscha finally relented on her one true wish. This is what Porscha Crisp Blogsnot then decided she wanted for her birthday:

New Lhasa apso

No more little brother (can't remember his name!)

Eyebrow and nasal surgery to look exactly like Aspen Judas!

And, most importantly: the Judas Brothers to play a concert in my very own backyard!!!

Shelley and Porscha presented this new, very fair request to Irving. Who blanched (*blanching* is when someone turns pale, like at the thought of bungee-jumping off Mount Everest or getting the Judas Brothers to play a concert in your backyard). They insisted I be present as a legal witness. Frankly, you couldn't pry me from this scene with a crowbar.

"Darling, sweetheart," he pleaded to Porscha, "the apple of Daddy's eye! Do you know how much a Judas Brothers concert would cost Papa?"

Porscha burst into tears. "Does this mean you won't be getting me my concert?" she cried.

"Irving!" Shelley said. "Look at our daughter—she's getting wrinkled from the crying. It's disgusting—how could you?!"

"How could you, Daddy!" Porscha yelled. Her new hot-pink Lhasa apso, Jo Jo, shuddered.

"Mom, Dad, what's going on?" L.V. asked, having wandered into Irving Blogsnot's mahogany-and-gold–trimmed office with giant palm trees in each corner.

"My God, L.V.!" Irving yelled. "Can't you see your sister is upset? How can you be so insensitive as to interrupt us?"

L.V.'s big eight-year-old eyes got even bigger. He blew his nose in his Mark Frost Academy (sponsored by Wild Pockets Banking, Ltd.) jacket sleeve. He wondered if he should tell his mom and dad—or Shelley and Irving, as they preferred to be called—about the straight A's he got on his report card. He wondered if he should tell them that his teacher said he was the smartest boy she'd ever had in second grade—he was reading at a ninth-grade level and he was already doing mathematical algorithms.

"L.V.," Shelley said, "I know you don't mean to be

cruel to your sister, but remember we went to the therapist about this? Remember what the therapist said?"

L.V. nodded his head slowly.

"'L.V.,' she said," Shelley repeated, "'your sister has an
artistic temperament, she's very, very fragile, she could
crack like an eggshell, or the skull of a baby bird dropped
from a high branch onto a hot sidewalk, and so we,
meaning you, have to be very careful with her feelings.'"

And that's when they had moved L.V.'s room to the
other side of the house.

L.V.'s old room had been converted into a monument
to the Judas Brothers. Porscha's parents bought up every
bit of Judas Brothers memorabilia on eBay they could
get their hands on. There were Jo Jo's old crib, Lukas's
third-grade artwork (a papier-mâché globe), and Aspen's
eyebrow clippings. There was a closet full of the Judas
Brothers' concert costumes—dating back to the first
time they sang in church. They tried to buy the Judas
Brothers' boyhood home and reconstruct it in their football field–sized backyard.

"For crying out loud, L.V.," Shelley said, "don't you

have anything else to do right now? Go . . . go do your . . . logorrodent things!" Shelley Blogsnot did not like having both her children in the room at the same time. She didn't like to be reminded that she was the mother of two—it made her feel old.

"Okay, Mom—but there's something . . . I got my grades—"

"L.V.!" Shelley said, exasperated. "How many times have I told you? My name is Shelley, I want to be called Shelley, not 'Mom.' And please, you know we don't want you harping on your grades in front of Porscha!"

"Mom!" Porscha wailed. "Why does he always have to harp on his grades? Why?"

"Sorry, Mom—I mean, Shelley," L.V. said while Porscha wailed.

"Please, L.V.," Irving said. "We're begging you— go . . . take your growth shots!"

And with that, tiny Irving Blogsnot closed his mahogany doors on little L.V. (who was actually taller than his father by now). And L.V. shook his little head (which was actually quite sizable and round).

One Week Later:

Irving Blogsnot had no luck booking the Judas Brothers for a backyard concert. He'd made phone calls, sent e-mails, IMs, and plaintive tweets. Nothing!

Meanwhile, poor little Porscha had lost all interest in eating and sleeping. Even more alarming, she'd lost all interest in shopping. (However, she did buy twelve scarves at the Abercrombie & Fitch website—four for each JB!) Even tiny dogs and big diamonds started to lose their charm for her. This is a short approximation of how the week went:

Tuesday: Porscha refused to eat.

Wednesday: Porscha refused to sleep!

Thursday: Porscha refused to bathe!

Friday: Porscha refused to shop!!

Saturday: Porscha refused to whine!!!

Sunday: Porscha refused to breathe!!!!

The therapist weighed in on speakerphone: The Blogsnots must follow little Porscha's interests and trust her judgment. At any cost.

Porscha, who had been put on a respirator and breathing tube—diamond-encrusted, natch—blinked her eyes in agreement. Tiny Irving Blogsnot nodded and slunk back into his office to make one more phone call. The entire family, including Porscha, lying on a gurney, waited outside his mahogany doors.

Finally, he swung open those doors, pulled up to his full height of just over five feet, and made an announcement: "I, Irving Blogsnot, have procured the Judas Brothers to play a concert for our precious Porscha in our very own backyard."

He only had to sell his soul and his yellow Ferrari to do it.

Porscha jumped off her gurney! Great news! Within

minutes, she was back to normal: eating, bathing, shopping, breathing, and treating everyone badly again! She only had one week to go before the concert! There was so so much to do! Plans must be made! People and dogs must be abused!

Everything had to be just right for the Judas Brothers! Porscha and Shelley geared up for the big day. This was the plan:

Send out invitations to all Porscha's friends at Mark Frost Academy (sponsored by Wild Pockets Banking, Ltd.).

Send out invitations to all Shelley's friends at the Ivy, the Polo Lounge, Neiman Marcus (fifth floor), Barneys New York shoe department, and the Beverly Hills Surgical Institute.

Send out invitations to all Irving's friends at the Creative International Agency, the Grill, and Club Fed (the penitentiary).

Find the same caterer who did the *Fast & Furious 18* premiere (the Judas Brothers love mini-burgers!).

To cut back on expenses, have L.V. and the gardener do the valet parking. There should be only three hundred cars, give or take.

Finally. The Big Day arrived.

But there was bad news: L.V., who studied meteorology in his spare time, tried to warn his parents that a rare Beverly Vista monsoon was wending its way up from the Gulf of Mexico.

Porscha, Shelley, and Irving didn't listen to L.V. They thought he was just trying to get out of valet parking three hundred cars. Even though he wasn't big enough to reach the gas pedal, he could manage!

The guests were to arrive at six o'clock.

They didn't.

By six thirty, a light rain had started to fall. I was in a rain slicker and boots, showing my support. And taking notes. And passing around mini-burgers on trays.

Hey, a buck is a buck.

And I did mention, did I not, that the Judas Brothers are super cute.

Meanwhile, Shelley was upset because of her hair—she hated frizz! She fired her hairdresser . . . but rehired him when she realized she'd fired every hairdresser in town.

By seven fifteen, there were still no guests. But there was a rainstorm. Shelley insisted, via walkie-talkie, that Antonio and L.V. remain waiting at the gate.

At seven thirty, a helicopter drifted over the rain-soaked backyard.

And landed.

Out hopped Aspen Judas, Lukas Judas, and Jo Jo Judas.

Porscha rushed the helicopter, narrowly missing the whirling blades. Lukas, the oldest, signaled Irving to come to the side for a conversation.

Over the booming of thunder and the crackle of lightning, Luke shouted out: "We have to cancel! It's too dangerous to play in this weather!"

"What weather, this?" Irving shouted above the

storm as drizzle dripped down his nose. "ABBA went on-stage in an Australian typhoon in '74!"

Porscha fainted from all the excitement. Shelley rushed to her side, but paused to have the photographer snap photos of her with all the JBs.

L.V., meanwhile, was bored. There were no cars to park, and he had been kind of looking forward to using his driving skills, once he found the gas pedal. He wandered into the backyard and went to check out the helicopter.

"Hey," Aspen said.

"Hey," said L.V.

"You think they're going to make us play?" Aspen asked.

L.V. looked at his dad, arguing with Lukas. Irving was winning. "Yes," he told Aspen, "I'm afraid so."

Porscha and Shelley escorted the Judas Brothers into their home to take lots of photos inside the JB Memorial Room.

The stage was set.

Lukas took his brothers aside. "Don't touch the

microphones, and you'll be okay," he told them. "Just sing."

They listened to him, nodding their heads and high-fiving. I fed them a few mini-burgers before their inevitable life-threatening injuries.

L.V. couldn't help but feel a twinge of jealousy when he watched the brothers do a group hug.

Porscha, Shelley, and Irving made themselves comfortable at the front of the stage. Porscha was grinning from ear to ear and vibrating with excitement. Every two seconds she let out a yelp. And she had already fainted three times from the stress! Her latest Lhasa apso, JB3, had run from her lap in fear for his life—every time she'd yelped, she'd squeezed him way too hard!

But L.V. couldn't take his eyes off the Judas family—he'd never had a group hug with his parents and sister.

Wait. He did have a pat on the head once.

Or was that a slap? He couldn't remember.

The Judas Brothers began singing as the rain continued to pour. They seemed perplexed that there wasn't anyone else there, but were energetic and enthusiastic.

They started off with "He Doesn't Even Know Your Shoe Size"—Porscha's very favorite song!

Halfway through the chorus, Aspen was wiggling his famous eyebrows and singing in his famous falsetto:

"He doesn't know-oh-oh,

He doesn't even know-oh-oh

Your shoooooe si-i-i—"

Suddenly, Porscha sprang from her seat and rushed the stage—she couldn't sit still during the chorus of her very favorite song on the whole planet from her very favorite member of her very favorite group of all time!

She pushed Aspen aside, grabbed the mike, and—

Oh.

Sparks shot out from the microphone. Porscha flew up in the air. Her hair spiraled from her head like an old-school 'fro. Her body lit up like a Christmas tree!

And then, just as quickly, Porscha dropped to the stage. The microphone rolled away from her, off the stage, and onto the grass.

The Judas Brothers stood back in horror. Aspen rushed over to Porscha. Steam was coming off her body as rain hit her forehead and sizzled off. Shelley and Irving rushed onto the stage.

Aspen, bending over Porscha, was shaking. "I think . . . I think she's . . ."

"Why did you stop playing?" Irving demanded.

Aspen looked up at them.

"Honey." Shelley bent over her daughter. "Honey, get up, you're missing everything!"

The photographer kept snapping photos of the scene.

"Irving!" Shelley yelled. "Tell Porscha this is not the time!"

"Now, listen here," Irving said to the Judas Brothers. "I paid for a concert, and I want a concert!"

"But, sir," Jo Jo said, "your daughter doesn't look too good—"

L.V. leapt up onstage and put his head to Porscha's sizzling chest.

"Call an ambulance," he yelled at Shelley.

"Don't you yell at me," Shelley said, then turned to the photographer, who was still snapping away. "Can you get one of me with the boys onstage?"

L.V. was already calling 911 on his cell phone—

although everyone knows the reception in Beverly Vista is not very good.

Meanwhile, Lukas Judas finally had enough. "Mister, I'm giving you your money back—you people are crazy!" Shelley kept taking photos with the stunned brothers.

"With interest!" Irving shouted.

L.V. turned to Lukas and started helping him pack up.

"You all right?" Lukas asked, putting a hand on the boy's shoulder.

"Yeah," L.V. said, looking back at his mother and father. "Hey, listen, I can't sing, but I can lift anything, and I've got determination and desire. I'd like to join you."

"What about your parents?" Lukas looked from L.V. to his parents, still making a fuss onstage. L.V. shrugged. "What does L.V. stand for, anyway?"

"It stands for . . ." L.V. was about to answer, then just shook his head. "Just call me Lou."

"'Kay, Lou—you need to pick up that speaker over there and put it on the 'copter."

"You got it."

And Lou picked up the speaker, which was very heavy, and grinned so hard, it hurt.

I raised my hand to say good-bye as the helicopter took off, swinging back and forth in the torrential rain amidst the distant howl of an ambulance.

L.V. put his hand to the window and smiled.

I've never seen a happier boy.

The End

WRATH

ometimes, even I, Perry Gonzales, feel sorry for myself. "Why don't I have a normal family?" I ask my mother, the R.N. "Why don't I have a father, a brother, a sister, a dog . . . a hamster? An espresso machine?"

(I'm just kidding about the espresso machine. But I would like a microwave. Just putting it out there.)

I've been told by my mother, the inestimable Yelena Maria Gonzales, that you can never really know what goes on in other people's households. That, in fact, the most normal family of all may be somewhat . . . abnormal.

Take the following domestic unit, for example. If you had driven by the Wankre (pronounced "WANK-ray") home on a sunny day, you would have seen Mr. Wankre, our ninth-grade bio teacher extraordinaire, watering the lawn; Mrs. Wankre, on her hands and knees, working in the garden; and the Wankre twins, almost-seven-year-old carrot-topped sprites named Mabel and Prudence, skipping rope in the front yard.

And then, if you were very observant, or very curious, or very nosy, or if your car was moving very, very slowly, you might have seen that Mr. Wankre's right arm was in a sling, Mrs. Wankre kept digging the same hole over and over (while muttering softly to herself), and the twins were not jumping rope, but were, in fact, fashioning nooses. You might also have noted that their practical Volvo sedan had four flat tires and a smashed taillight.

And if your senses were sharp as a bat at night or the tip of a rattlesnake's forked tongue, you might have caught the stream of black smoke coming out of the chimney. You might have felt the earth shift ever so slightly. You might have heard crashing sounds and a wild animal—no, a wild, prehistoric monster—bellowing from inside.

And you would know, in an instant, that this "normal house" with this "normal family" was not so normal after all.

What was not-so-normal about the Wankres?

Meet William Wankre. (If I have to, you have to.) From outward appearances, William was a robust, red-headed, red-faced, twelve-almost-thirteen-year-old boy who lived in a nice suburban neighborhood in a nice house in a sunny climate with his nice parents and his very nice twin sisters, almost-seven-year-old Prudence and Mabel. William's dad, Mr. Wankre, was my favorite science teacher at Mark Frost Academy; Mrs. Wankre was a stay-at-home mom.

Mr. Wankre had approached me after biology class one afternoon to ask if I'd be interested in watching his twin girls for a few hours a week.

Well, at first he said, in his warbly voice, "Perry, I'm hearing good things about your tutoring business. You're gaining quite the rep with the more, er, difficult personalities we have here. Would you be interested in guarding my girls so my wife can nap for just a few minutes, if it's not too much trouble?"

His face, covered in stubble, was pale behind his glasses, which had been broken and taped together above his nose. I noticed that he'd become more gaunt, his cheeks more sunken, in the few months I'd known him.

"Guard your girls? From what, Mr. Wankre?" I asked.

"Oh, ah, did I say 'guard'? I meant babysit," he blurted out. His lip quivered. "I'd like you to babysit my girls for an hour here or there . . ."

◆━━▶━━◆

In a soft, breathy voice with a hint of the Southern belle she once was, Mrs. Wankre sat in her living room and explained little William's "eccentricities" to me while he played video games in the next room. The twins were still in after-school activities.

I couldn't help but notice various holes in the walls, the ripped sofa cushions.

What I could have sworn were bloodstains on the area rug.

Mrs. Wankre told me she used to be known as Dr. Wankre. She had a bustling career as a pediatrician in a lovely red-brick building. She even had her own brass nameplate on the door. Oh, she dearly loved taking care of children—encouraging toddlers to listen to their bodies with her stethoscope, bouncing babies on her knee, counseling middle school kids about bullies and hormones—but she was forced to quit when William was a tot.

"I don't want to alarm you," she said, absentmindedly fingering the stethoscope she still wore around her neck. "But our little William has been quite the, er, challenge."

Mrs. Wankre had become increasingly frightened in her once cozy household—and for good reason. Little William's bad moods were becoming bad reality TV (hi, oxymoron!).

In a voice so quiet, I was forced to lean in, Mrs. Wankre rattled off the following:

1. When William Wankre was a teeny, tiny baby, he chomped on the pet cat's tail repeatedly (he had his first tooth at three weeks, a full set at three months!), until the cat and his bloodied tail finally went to live under the house.

2. William was an early walker. He walked at five months on tree-stump legs. Which would have been exciting, except he used those legs to kick holes in the plaster in the TV room. He did this when Mrs. Wankre refused to let him watch R-rated movies, like *Blade* and *Scarface*.

3. Mrs. Wankre was run out of the local park, even at night, because of little William. She was ejected from two shopping malls (and a Williams-Sonoma). The aquarium has her on a no-entry list. Five minutes into interviews, she was not allowed to enroll William in several nursery schools.

Why? Foul language. (See the above-referenced "favorite movies.") William, apparently, could bring a blush to Kanye's cheek, and a "oh, no, he di'n't!" to his mouth.

On a bright Monday morning, a little over seven years ago, Mrs. Wankre found out she was pregnant—with twin girls! She kept this wonderful news secret from William until one afternoon, the postman asked how she was "coming along" and when she was "due."

And that's when little William rolled up his little hand (he was already over forty pounds and eating steak for breakfast) into a fist and punched Mrs. Wankre right in her Mabel-and-Prudence tummy. (Mabel and Prudence would swear to you, if they actually talked, that they still remember being knocked around—and this is why they had to be coaxed out of their mother's womb a whole three weeks late!)

Mrs. Wankre would try to control her little boy. Mr. Wankre would try to control his little boy.

They tried:

1. Cajoling
2. Encouraging

3. Ferberizing
4. Yelling and screaming
5. Brazeltoning
6. Buying (things)
7. Bribing with food
8. Bribing with sleep times
9. Sleep aids (only once, and they have fond memories)
10. That collar for dogs that have undergone surgery

All to no avail. When the twins came along, William Wankre was ready for them. Mr. and Mrs. Wankre slept with the twins next to their bed in matching bassinets for as long as possible. Mrs. Wankre caught William sneaking into their bedroom holding a pillow above his head.

After that, Mr. and Mrs. Wankre took turns sleeping.

Finally, when Mrs. Wankre found a kitchen knife stowed in William's overnight diaper, the Wankres quickly decided that one of them would have to stay home full-time in order to keep William from slicing and dicing, suffocating or damaging in any way his brand-new baby sisters.

Mrs. Wankre immediately gave up her kid patients and her beloved practice.

◆━◆━◆

I can't explain why, and I don't expect you to believe it, but little William (who was much bigger, taller, stronger, and meaner than I) did not scare me.

Maybe because of where I grew up. My apartment building borders two opposing gangs. An Armenian gang—they tend to be short and squat and have facial hair at nine years old, drive refurbished Camaros, and have small, crooked teeth. The second gang is El Salvadoreño—they tend to be short and stringy and have no facial hair until they are in their thirties. They drive refurbished El Caminos and have coal black, greasy 'dos. There is a line drawn down the middle of our street and no welcome mats on either side.

(Keep in mind, there are numerous Armenian and Latino gang subsets—these are just my friendly neighborhood ones.)

I'd stopped jumping at the report of occasional gunfire when I was still wearing jumpers. I learned to ask questions with my ears, my skin, and my eyes, not my lips.

So this man-child who barreled into the Wankre living room, with his corona of orange hair and constellation of freckles (extra credit for astronomy metaphors?), would have to come with it, if you know what I mean.

Mrs. Wankre had told me to stand very still when she introduced us. Sudden movements enraged little William.

Sometimes, breathing enraged little William.

(Little William was sounding like a laugh riot.)

Still, my curiosity (my mother would say "nosiness") had gotten the best of me. A good story is a good story, even if I have to lose an ear to get it.

William immediately started sniffing me. It was not unlike being assaulted by a Great Dane with a personality disorder. Mrs. Wankre had warned me that he could smell fear.

I stared him down. Somewhere, sometime, I had learned that Tom Cruise, the famous Scientologist/movie star, does not blink during interviews. If Tom could do it, I could do it.

"Get out of my house," he growled. "You smell like taquitos."

"Hi, William. I'm Perry," I said, unwavering. "And your mother is going to sleep now."

"SHUT UP!" he bellowed.

Despite the molten hotness of his breath upon my face, I stood my ground.

"Mrs. Wankre, go take your nap," I said, my eyes on Mad Ginger. "William and I are going to play a game."

"GET OUT!"

"Go ahead, Mrs. Wankre. I got this."

And to my surprise, Mrs. Wankre, shaking though she was, tiptoed past her son to her bedroom and closed the door.

And locked it, which was worrisome.

William's face turned bright red. He picked up a chair and threw it against the front door.

"Boring," I said, and I brought out my handy pack of cards, good for any babysitting occasion. "Are you afraid to play me in a game? Crazy Eights?"

"I'LL KILL YOU!"

"You don't like Crazy Eights. Gin Rummy?"

William screamed.

"Ah, so you *are* afraid. Okay. We'll just read, then."

I sat down with a book I'd been meaning to finish— no, not *The Hunger Games*. The other one. I didn't flinch as William ran at his mother's door, throwing his shoulder into it and cracking it from its hinges; I didn't blink when he rolled on the floor and gnawed on a chair leg. I yawned when he punched his fist through the television set.

I finished the last chapter as he lay on the floor, panting and wheezing from exhaustion.

I checked my watch.

"Well, that went quickly," I said.

"I HATE YOU!" he yelled from the floor.

"Let me go wake up your mom," I said as I skipped over him. "We'll continue the fun in a few days."

The next week, Mrs. Wankre introduced me to Prudence and Mabel. The girls were white as paper, with bones like birds, tiny pink mouths, cornflower blue eyes, and strawberry bobs. They curtsied, blinked quickly for ten seconds, and sat down for tea at a small round table, motioning for me to sit with them.

After sipping tea and exchanging shy smiles, I noticed that neither of them had said a word. I asked them questions and they smiled. That was it. Somehow, though, I understood their answers. I told them a bit about myself. They smiled and nodded, eager to hear more.

That's when I asked them, "Mabel? Prudence? Do you girls talk?"

Prudence and Mabel looked at each other, blinked, and looked back at me—four round blue eyes saying *no*.

And *What's the point?*

I grinned and put my hands out for them to hold.

As they've since explained to me in elaborate baroque script—they are already expert calligraphers—here are a few more things the Wankres have tried over the years to help William:

1. Homeopathic medicine
2. Horse-petting
3. Meditation
4. Exercise
5. Macrobiotic diet
6. Dogs and fish, but not together
7. A meeting with Gwyneth Paltrow (in which he tried to bite part of her ear off)
8. Any psychological guru with a funny accent
9. Oprah.com
10. Therapy

The first therapist said the Wankres should listen more. She quit after William burned a hole through her couch with a lighter he picked up in Vegas. The second therapist said William needed extra hugs. She quit after he hugged her and left a scar. A third therapist suggested electroshock therapy, but William was too young. The Wankres then tried lying about his age to the therapist.

11. Botox (for Mrs. Wankre, for all her worry lines)

A typical day in the Wankre household? Mom and Dad would put on their padded body suits under their normal, everyday clothes. The girls, thus far, had refused to wear pads—but then, they were considerably faster on their feet than Mom and Dad Wankre.

Every morning, William woke up bellowing like something out of *Jurassic Park*, threw his oatmeal at his mother, monkey-bit his sisters, taunted them when they cried out, emptied his lunch on the floor and stomped on his meat sandwich, then ripped up his father's newspaper and pushed him aside as he rushed out to the bus stop in order to be on time to terrorize the schoolbus driver, Anita.

And that was all before eight a.m.

There were many things the Wankre family hadn't done because of Willie Wankre's, er, "special" behaviors. They'd never: had a peaceful meal; gone on a family vacation; attended the circus, or a sporting event, or a birthday party (forget about Christmas, Hanukkah, or Kwanzaa parties!). They'd never even taken a quiet walk around the block.

They had: dodged flying plates, cups, and silverware; used trash can lids to parry makeshift swords; learned how to patch a nailed tire with duct tape and spit; hidden the knives; hidden the forks; become very good at something called "triage"; created earplugs out of snot and bits of paper in ten seconds or less; worked themselves up to extraordinary foot speeds (in the case of the twins).

At school, William Wankre was even worse. He was, as you can imagine, a huge bully. He was over six feet tall. He was even bigger than the school principal. He was much bigger than his teachers. He may even have been bigger than Shaq (though Shaq seems very nice and not at all like William Wankre).

In his sixth-grade classroom, Willie burped and farted and made belching noises during other pupils' oral book reports. His own book report was a series of farts and burps made to sound like the Gettysburg Address.

Homeschooling became the only alternative.

The principal's tic is just starting to go away.

⬥———◄▶———⬥

On Prudence and Mabel's birthday, their fondest wish was for a hamster. They had begged Mr. and Mrs. Wankre for a hamster since as far back as they could remember—both telepathically and in writing. Every night, their thoughts turned to prayers for a hamster. And every morning, they spelled out *hamster* with their breakfast cereal.

Mr. and Mrs. Wankre had tried to explain to the girls, whom they knew to be reasonable and sensitive, why they couldn't have a pet. Now, at this point in the story, you may not think of Prudence and Mabel as reasonable and sensitive. You may think of them as weird. You may think of them as freaks. *Why don't these girls talk?* you might ask. *Why don't they just use their voice boxes and their vocal cords like any other reasonable and sensitive seven-year-old twins?*

Well, as they've explained to me, if you lived in a house where one voice was one hundred times louder than all the others combined, would you just not try anymore? Would you still use your voice?

Maybe. And maybe not.

When Prudence and Mabel were babies, being reasonable and sensitive infants, they knew what they were in for. They heard every loud remark, burp, utterance, yell, scream, fart, and holler coming out of their big brother William's various orifices. In fact, while Prudence and Mabel were still in Mrs. Wankre's tummy and barely even had fully formed ears, they made a pact to communicate in ways that couldn't be breached.

Instead of using their mouths to converse, they decided they would use their brain waves.

They were very, very smart tiny little babies.

But let's not dwell. Back to the hamster dilemma.

The girls wanted a hamster; Mr. and Mrs. Wankre were dubious. They didn't even want to remind William that the girls' birthday was coming up, because he'd ruin it—as he did, consistently, every year.

In what ways had he ruined Prudence and Mabel's birthdays?

Year One: William sat on their birthday cake.

Year Two: William ran the car over their matching tricycles.

Year Three: William spit in the fruit punch.

Year Four: William peed in the fruit punch.

Year Five: I won't tell you what William did to the fruit punch that year.

Year Six: Mabel and Prudence refused to celebrate their birthday.

Year Seven: WHO KNOWS WHAT WOULD HAPPEN IF THEY GOT A HAMSTER?

I shudder to think.

There was the time the Wankres got a round, wiggly

puppy, thinking that maybe what young William needed was a pet to love.

William squeezed the puppy.

And squeezed it.

And squeezed it.

And just as it looked like there would be a puppy explosion, Mrs. Wankre tickled William hard under his arms. William released the puppy, and the puppy—whose name was Puppy, because they never figured out a better name, because they didn't actually own him for more than twenty minutes—ran away and was never seen nor heard from again.

Mabel and Prudence, in addition to being reasonable and sensitive, had animal telepathy—if they knew where Puppy ran off to, they would never tell. They also read many psychology books like *Your Difficult Sibling* or *Essentials of Abnormal Psychology*. They advised their parents—who were, after all the aforementioned efforts, at a complete loss—on how to treat their older brother by highlighting pertinent passages. Poor Mrs. Wankre wore a wig—she hardly had any hair left from pulling it out—and Mr. Wankre hardly had any teeth left from grinding at night.

I did my best to give Mrs. Wankre a break for a couple hours a week, but frankly, that boy was not getting any better, and may have been getting worse.

One night, when I came home from the Wankre house with a bruise on my forehead (flying I ♥ ATLANTA coffee mug), my mother put her small foot down.

I told Mr. Wankre, my voice filled with regret, that I would not be able to babysit/guard/dodge flying mugs anymore. I was giving two weeks' notice.

He nodded, his long face longer and sadder, and gave me a hug.

Prudence and Mabel (who finished each other's sentences in each other's heads) showed their mother an article regarding a new wonder drug that might just work on Willie's temper. Mrs. Wankre was against drugs (except for the homeopathic ones that don't work), but since Willie had that incident with the local sheriff and the Taser, she was willing to give it a try.

Willie was put on the wonder drug. And at first, it

appeared to do nothing. And then, an extremely weird thing happened: William became normal. And he stayed normal. For a whole week! The family went out to dinner. They went to see a movie. The kids played tag in the front yard—and Willie didn't trip, hit, punch, or kick the twins! Willie pet a dog. Mr. and Mrs. Wankre bought Prudence and Mabel a pet hamster, Mr. Heywood. Mrs. Wankre's hair even started growing back. All was well! Ding-dong, the Wankre was dead!

After a week, Willie felt so normal that he started skipping his dosages. He decided he didn't need the drug anymore—and what's more, he didn't even like it.

William liked being angry. He liked being in control of his household. He liked seeing fear in people's eyes. He wasn't comfortable feeling "normal." Normal was for nimrods. Willie Wankre wanted respect! Willie Wankre wanted power!

Willie went back to being a terror, only MUCH MORE so than before. He was angrier and bigger and redder and meaner than he ever was. Mrs. Wankre was near bald, and Mr. Wankre had to suck his food through a straw. Not even Prudence and Mabel knew what to do next.

Their conversation (from behind their bolted door) went something like this:

"What do we do now?"

"I don't know, Pru. What do we do?"

"I don't know, Mabel—what do you think we should do?"

The girls took to sitting with their backs against each other at breakfast (so they could watch for flying objects), and their brains talked back and forth while they ate.

As dishes flew and oatmeal whizzed by, they came up with a most amazing plan.

What is Willie Wankre's favorite food? Hot dogs!

He loved hot dogs. The girls offered to make hot dogs for dinner while their mom took some much-needed rest.

In the meantime, the girls snuck into Willie's bathroom to "borrow" their brother's medication—dangerous, indeed, because he could find them there . . .

Which he did.

But before he had a chance to throw a tennis shoe at their heads or give them hard noogies or monkey bites, Prudence and Mabel acted like they were busily cleaning his room.

So Willie calmed down. A bit.

But guess what? As he sat down to his hot dog meal (in his room, where he wanted it), he decided that they should clean his room every day—and wash his dirty underwear!

The girls had brought him four hot dogs on a TV tray, with the mustard, ketchup, and relish already on— just how he liked it! (And to cover the taste of the . . .)

"What's that funny aftertaste?" Willie demanded, while the girls watched and shook in their boots.

"Um . . . it's a different kind of relish?" Prudence suggested (in her brain). From outward appearances, she merely shrugged.

"Mmrgh. I like it," Willie grunted, ignoring her.

The girls giggled and shook. (But they didn't giggle too, too loudly.)

"I want more!" Willie yelled.

The girls looked at each other.

"More?" they asked him with their eyes.

"Yes, more!" Willie screamed. "Now!"

The girls scrambled and brought more hot dogs into Willie's room, where he was now playing his favorite video game, Grand Theft Killing Machine Bloodlust Guns 'n' Stuff Volume IV.

Willie took a bite. "Where's the special relish?!" he demanded, then threw the hot dog against the wall.

The girls looked at each other.

"I want the special relish!" Willie screamed.

The girls bit their lips.

"Now!" Willie yelled.

"Special relish on the way," the girls said in their heads.

The girls made a half dozen more dogs. All with that "special relish."

"I'm sleepy," Willie said after eating the whole lot. "Take my plate away."

And then Willie lay his big, giant, red head down.

And fell asleep. Snorting and snoring like a bear.

The girls watched him. Then tiptoed away.

And in the morning, the house was quiet. Willie was still sleeping—and snorting.

They tried to wake him. Clapping their hands, then poking him gently. Then a bit harder. Nothing.

Mr. Wankre clapped in his ear. Then yelled. Nothing.

Mrs. Wankre started to cry, although the girls weren't sure if she was relieved or anxious.

The ambulance came.

The girls tried to tell their parents what they'd done (grinding his pills with their heels and mixing them in with the relish—a not unpleasant adventure), but Mr. and Mrs. Wankre were too crazed to listen.

The hospital couldn't quite figure it out. He was in a coma, that was for sure, but a very, very loud one. They took his blood and found out he'd overdosed on his medication. His parents were horrified—but heartened by the fact that he wanted to go back on it! *That's so sweet! So considerate!*

The girls trembled while their brains had a conversation. It went something like this:

"Uh-oh."

"Yes, uh-oh."

"Maybe we should have fed him a little every day."

"Didn't we vote on this?"

"Yes."

"The democratic process was served, correct?"

"Yes, of course."

"Well, then, we'll just live with the consequences."

"The doctor smells like turpentine."

"Let's go see the other patients."

"Right."

(Prudence was one minute older than Mabel, which made her the boss, but not the leader. Or the leader, but not the boss.)

Willie eventually came out of his snorting, snoring coma and was brought home by his loving parents. He is now a shadow of his former self. Meaning William is nice. Really nice. He takes pleasure in the simple things. He talks softly and slowly and he smiles. He smiles a lot, and sometimes he claps when something strikes him as funny.

He sits quietly when I read to him.

He loves playing Crazy Eights and Go Fish.

He is going to be this way for a very, very long time. Perhaps, the doctors say, for the rest of his life.

They are very sorry, those doctors. It's a tragedy, they say.

The Wankres nod. *Oh yes, a tragedy.*

The Wankre family enjoys going out to dinner. And the movies. And Disneyland. And eating breakfast. And Mrs. Wankre has started working part-time as a pediatrician, where she bounces babies on her knee and encourages toddlers to play with her stethoscope.

Mr. Wankre has gotten another pair of glasses and gained a few pounds.

And the young Wankre twins enjoy dressing their big brother up in girl clothes and playing teatime with him. Willie giggles when the girls comb his hair, and he enjoys their teas immensely. The girls have become so relaxed, they've even started mouthing words like *please* and *thank you.*

Mr. Heywood comes out of hiding in Prudence and Mabel's clothes hamper. Willie Wankre sleeps with Mr. Heywood at night, and he is very careful not to roll over on him.

The End

GLUTTONY

B y now, my dear Admissions Committee, you
have grown accustomed to meeting strange
characters—but there is none so strange as
Angus Willhelm (pronounced "VIL-h-eye-m").
Prepare yourselves.

Little Angus lived in an apartment with his mother in
a special part of Southern California known as "the Valley" (pronounced "WALL-ee"). Angus's mom, Mrs. Willhelm, was not married, and there was no Mr. Willhelm.

Mystery Alert: Mr. Willhelm vanished under suspi-
cious circumstances when Angus was a baby. Suffice it to
say, they've never found a body—but crumbs from a Jiffy

corn muffin (Mr. Willhelm's favorite) were found on the side of a freeway overpass. Cue ominous music, heavy on the oboe.

Mrs. Willhelm (pronounced "VEEL-home") promptly moved baby Angus and herself into their tidy apartment building called Via Toscana (though it's nowhere near Italy) on a nondescript (which means "not special") street called La Rosa Drive (Spanish for *rose*, though no roses grow on La Rosa).

Mrs. Willhelm (pronounced "VUL-chum") valued cleanliness above all things, which was why she and the baby had to move quickly from their home right after Mr. Willhelm (pronounced "VAL-ham") disappeared, because there appeared an enormous bloodstain on the living room carpet. No matter how hard she scrubbed and bleached and scrubbed some more, Mrs. Willhelm could not get the spot out!

Who could live under such circumstances?

Mrs. Willhelm (don't worry, I'll end the pronouncements) made sure that no germs ever touched her little Ang-y. She gave him twenty-two baths a day, wiped his hands constantly with—what else—Handi Wipes, used hand sanitizer as shampoo, and put him in a hazmat suit when he ventured outside. Because Mrs. Willhelm never wanted Angus to put his feet on the ground, as even her sparkling floors could be harboring flesh-eating bacteria, she encouraged him to eat and eat and eat so he'd be too fat to walk when the time came.

And the time came . . . and went.

This is Angus at six months. (Clever illustration.)

This is Angus at ten months.

This is Angus at twelve months (when he should have been walking!).

You see, he was shaped like a beach ball—a squeaky-clean beach ball. He weighed 120 pounds at one year of age and couldn't possibly support his weight on his chubby little stumps.

Mrs. Willhelm (pronounced—whoops!) eventually went back to work as a nurse when her poor departed poisoned and mortally wounded (which means "stabbed with a kitchen knife") husband's life insurance ran out. By that time, Angus was five years old, and there was no way Mrs. Willhelm was going to allow him to go to kindergarten.

Angus didn't want to go to kindergarten. His mother had told him that other kids were full of awful germs, and if he went and they wiped their hideous snot-filled noses on his round cheeks, his nose would start bleeding, his ears would start ringing, and he would throw up his breakfast (twelve fried eggs, three packs of Jimmy Dean sausage, a ten-stack of frozen pancakes, and one quart of that orange juice that's 11 percent juice and 89 percent battery acid) and die a horrible death!

Well, Angus would have none of it. He could learn everything he wanted from life from watching snack food commercials. He learned words like *juicy*, *sweet*, *salty*, and *hydrogenated*. He learned to look for words like *high-fructose corn syrup* on labels—because that's the flavor he liked best! Red dye #3 was a strong second, Fiery Red-Hot Swizzle Chips a sassy third.

As it turned out, Angus was a very bright boy, and by second grade (or what should have been second grade, for Angus was still not enrolled in school), young Angus had worked out a very elaborate system for deciding what he would eat on any given day, and at which fifteen-minute intervals. A surprise TV commercial could send him into fits, though—because he'd have to rejigger (this means "adapt" or "change") the Angus Eating Schedule system to prevent the nefarious and fearful Blood Sugar Drop.

Oh? You've never heard of the nefarious and fearful Blood Sugar Drop?

Well, time for a little science lesson. I'll let Dr. Sigmundus Broatius, for the study of the incorrigible BSD at the Institute of Digestive Disorders, third floor (sponsored by Nabisco), www.nefariousandfearfulbloodsugar drop.org, take the floor.

In other words, I'll let him explain in detail.

Dr. Sigmundus Broatius

(speaking loudly, with an Austrian accent):

Yessss, normal blood glucose levels are about 90mg/ 100ml, equivalent to 5mM (mmol/l) (as molecular weight of glucose, $C_6H_{12}O_6$ is about 180g/mol daltons). The total amount of glucose normally in circulating human blood is therefore about 3.3 to 7g

(assuming an ordinary adult blood volume of 5 litres,

plausible for an average adult male—

Thank you, Dr. Broatius! That's quite enough!

Bottom line? If Little Angus didn't eat every fifteen minutes, on the minute, he would get into a very foul funk. And he would stay in his foul funk until his next blueberry muffin.

This was a typical day in Angus's young life:

Angus would roll out of bed and onto the floor just before noon; he woke up late because he was watching his plasma HD television set until four in the morning. (Angus sometimes had blurred vision caused by his BSD, and he needed a picture that was pinpoint clear.)

Twelve noon: Precisely at noon, Angus would eat an entire box of Entenmann's mini cinnamon buns with the icing on top. He would lick the icing off each bun first, and then eat the bun.

This got him off to a good start.

And then, while watching television, he would pick up his banjo and cobble together a ditty. Angus's biggest goal in life was to write theme songs for crunchy, sweet, and salty snacks. Here's his latest:

I think that I shall never see
a jewel as lovely as a three-
package bag of hot 'chitos!

Angus had a lovely singing voice.

Every fifteen minutes, Angus would eat a sugary starch or fatty protein, followed by an energy bar.

Every thirty minutes, he would drink diet soda or a vitamin drink.

Every forty-five minutes, he would drink a Coke to make up for the diet soda.

Six p.m.: Angus would be hungry for dinner. If it was Monday, Mrs. Willhelm would bring home McDonald's; if it was Tuesday, it was KFC. Wednesdays were for Burger King, Thursdays belonged to Pizza Hut, Friday wouldn't have been Friday without Panda Express, Saturday was Taco Bell's big day (*olé!*), and Sunday, the Sabbath, a day for introspection, was the perfect time to dive into a Blimpie or two. Or three. Or eight.

GIGI LEVANGIE

This routine went on for years.

One fateful day, Mother Willhelm, who was getting older, couldn't put on her nurse's shoes—she couldn't even take another step. Her bunions were causing so much pain that she had to have them removed. Mrs. Willhelm's doctor told her she had to spend the night in the hospital, and so must leave her beloved son, Angus, in the care of a babysitter.

Angus was not happy about this at all—he'd never had a babysitter in his life! Why would he need a babysitter when he had his trusty plasma television set and mini-fridge?

But Mrs. Willhelm put her foot down (gingerly). She hired me, Perry Gonzales, the daughter of her coworker and head nurse, Yelena Maria Gonzales, to watch Angus for one night.

Now, I consider myself an expert babysitter. At fourteen, I've already got six years of experience under my belt; I've never met a ward (that means "child") I couldn't A. entertain or B. control.

Until I met Angus.

At first, I was shocked. I thought I was babysitting a normal eleven-year-old boy.

"You'll love Angus," Mrs. Willhelm had told me. "He's just a charmer!"

But nothing about this boy looked . . . charming. First of all, he was enormously fat—fatter than any child I have ever seen. Or any full-grown adult, for that matter. Secondly, he was a giant—his feet and hands were huge.

I took one look at Angus and crossed myself. *"Ay, Dios mío,"* I said.

Which means, basically, "Oh, crap."

Angus couldn't hear me—*iCarly* was on way too loud. I looked more closely at him: He had a banjo on his lap, wrapped up in his girth. And he appeared to be swaddled in a large diaper.

His sausage fingers picked out a tune while his eyes stayed glued to the set.

A cat flitted by.

"Angus?" I called out as I stepped across a sea of candy wrappers and soda cans.

"Leave me alone, Mom!" Angus said, without turn-

2151

ing his head, in a high-pitched squeal. Then he pressed the mute button on the remote and picked out a tune on his banjo. I watched in awe as he sang:

A corny can of Cheezy Whip—
You'll want your fingers in to dip.
And Mom will say, "Now that's enough,"
But you can't get enough o' that STUFF!

And then, Angus let out a large BURP.

He looked over at me. I was stunned. Angus had a beautiful falsetto. But it came out of *that* mouth, which was part of *that* face!

The face looked like a large, white bowling ball with piercing onyx eyes and a teeny-tiny turned-up nose. His lips were bowed and had a red tinge. He had one blond curl at the top of his round head. He looked like a baby doll that had soaked up a bathtub full of water.

Make that a swimming pool.

"Who are you?" Angus whined. "Where's my MOM?"

"Your mother is having an operation," I said, gathering my wits. "My name is Perry. And I will be babysitting you tonight. Your mother does not want you to be alone. As you can see by my résumé," I continued, handing over my résumé, which I always keep on hand, "I am a professional, and I am here to either A. entertain you or B. control you—the choice is up to you."

"I don't like you!" Angus wheezed. "Get me my energy bars!"

"What's the magic word?" I asked, looking about the messy room.

"Mooooooooooom!" Angus squealed.

"Your mother's away," I said calmly. "The magic word is *please*."

Angus burped, then screamed, "You're making me miss *America's Next Top Model*!" Angus moved his body ever so gingerly. "Now, get me an energy bar! I feel DIZZY!" His chair creaked as he reached for the remote.

I snatched the remote away. "Use the word. The magic one," I said calmly.

Angus raised his hand and pointed a very chubby finger at me.

"I don't like you!" he squealed again.

"That's fine," I said. "Let's have a pleasant conversation. Then I'll let you go back to your show. How was school today?"

"I don't go to school," Angus said. "Germs go to school."

"Everyone goes to school," I said.

"I don't!" Angus screamed. "I'm too smart to go to school! Ask Mom!"

"But how do you learn?" I asked, genuinely puzzled.

"TV!" Angus said. "I'm missing my program!" He leaned forward and tried to grab the remote, brushing the air with his chubby arms and falling right on the floor.

"You made me fall!" he screamed as he rolled around in his diaper, candy wrappers sticking to his big, sweaty body.

I stepped back quickly. "I'll help you up. And then we are going to have a conversation before you watch television. School isn't just about getting smarter. School is about socialization skills. And apparently, you don't have any."

Angus lay on the floor, trying to sit up, but having no luck. He could, however, get his head off the floor if he tried very, very hard. He grunted and rolled over onto his belly.

I watched Angus writhing and mewling like a walrus that couldn't maneuver off an ice floe. And that's when I realized: This boy could be my greatest calling, my greatest gift. I, Perry Gonzales, had trained every week since the fourth grade for this moment.

I would help Angus. I would change his life for the better. I would . . . make him take a walk.

I put my hand out to help him up.

And Angus reached out . . . grabbed my hand . . . and bit me!

"Ow!" I yelled, and dropped the remote control as I yanked my arm back. A fine trickle of blood was starting to drip from my skinny forearm to my little finger.

The cat, an orange tabby, flitted around my legs, then looked up at me with a sorry expression. In my shock, I saw a warning expression in its emerald eyes.

Get out while you can, the cat seemed to be saying.

Angus had rolled over on his back, wriggled over to the chair, and was now resting against it. He was watching me, smiling.

And then Angus licked his lips.

"How dare you bite me?" I lost my temper, I'm sorry to say. This was the first time I raised my voice at a client, ever. "You're not allowed to go around biting people!"

"I can if they don't give me my remote!" Angus whined. "And I'm hungry and you're not feeding me and I'm telling my mom!"

I cleared a chair and sat down. "Have you had your shots?" I asked, inspecting my wound.

"No!" Angus said. "I don't need any shots! I don't have GERMS!"

I went into the bathroom, which was quite neat compared to the living room, and washed my arm with soap and water and hydrogen peroxide (Mrs. Willhelm had twenty bottles under the sink). There were two half circles of teeth marks; Angus had broken the skin.

I covered the wound with bandages and made a note to ask my mom about a rabies shot first thing tomorrow morning. But before that, I still had a job to do.

While Angus whined about missing his program, I set about making a healthy dinner. Which was kind of difficult—there was no fresh food in the cupboard. The refrigerator was stocked with Lunchables, ranch dressing, and strawberry lemonade.

Luckily, I always carry healthy snacks with me to my jobs. I made a fresh vegetable platter with raw carrots, broccoli, and cauliflower florets and used the ranch dressing as a dip.

And set it out for Angus to eat.

"I won't eat that crap!" he squealed, staring at the vegetables. "What if I choke?"

"You don't eat, you don't watch," I said, grabbing the remote and waving it above my head.

Angus relented. He tasted the vegetables and made disgusting noises with each bite. He spit out pieces of broccoli and wiped the remnants on his chest.

But he finished the plate.

And I turned on the television set.

When I wasn't looking, I felt like Angus was sneaking peeks at the wound on my arm.

And licking his lips.

That night, I slept in the Willhelm apartment— behind the locked door of Mrs. Willhelm's bedroom—

and had vampire dreams. In the morning, I noticed the cat was missing.

"Angus," I asked, "do you know where the cat is? I need to feed it before I leave for school."

Angus gave me a strange look. "What cat?" he asked in his high-pitched voice.

I shook my head. The cat bowl was empty—so the cat had eaten its dinner. I left some water out.

"Are you going to be okay?" I asked before I left. I was relieved to be going. "I can't be late to school."

"Yes," Angus replied. "I'm fine. Thank you."

I looked up at Angus, shocked. He was being polite; what was that about? I didn't know why—but his tone gave me chills.

That evening, Mother Willhelm came back to the apartment she shared with Angus. Her foot was in a cast, and she was in a foul mood. She'd been called by the school authorities. Angus had to be enrolled in school— the following day!

"Angus, what did you do to Perry?" Mrs. Willhelm asked. She hobbled over to where Angus was sitting, banjo in his lap. "The authorities called me today at the hospital—I was still in bed, recovering!"

"Why'd you leave me, Mother?" Angus squealed. "She was so awful! She made me eat roughage!"

"Did you bite Perry?" Mrs. Willhelm asked. "She had to report you to the school nurse. Perry had to get shots."

"I didn't bite her!" Angus lied. "She snatched the remote from my mouth! It was an accident!"

Mrs. Willhelm took one long, sad look at her son.

"Angus," Mrs. Willhelm said as she sat down. Her cast made it hard for her to move, and dragging her foot around had tired her out. "Darling. My love. I've had some time to think. And I'm afraid I've done you a grave disservice. It is time you went to school. You have to learn manners. You have to learn to get along with other kids. Maybe you'll catch a cold, diphtheria, bird flu, or Ebola, but maybe not. Tomorrow morning, you and I will go down to the school and enroll you."

"NO!" Angus screamed. "I can't go to school! There's GERMS in school!"

"Angus, I'm sorry," Mrs. Willhelm said. "But if you

don't go to school, Mommy will be arrested—and then who will take care of you?"

"You can't make me go to school! I won't do it!" Angus yelled.

"I'm going to bed now, Angus." His mother sighed, then looked around the room. "Where's the tabby?"

"It ran off when Perry opened the door," he squealed, and shrugged.

Mrs. Willhelm just shook her head. "Good night, Angus," she said. "Sweet dreams. Oh, and starting tomorrow, I think it wouldn't hurt for both of us to start eating more vegetables. It's time for the Willhelms to go on a diet."

That night, Mrs. Willhelm had terrible dreams. Vampires, werewolves, and spider monkeys all made guest appearances in her nightmares.

At four a.m., she woke up to find Angus standing next to her bed.

"Angus!" Mrs. Willhelm said, sitting up in her flannel nightie with her bonnet on. "You startled me. H-how did you manage to get in here?"

"I don't want to eat vegetables, Mom," Angus whined.

"I hate vegetables. I need protein to grow! I need protein to feel good!"

"Angus, we'll talk about this in the morning," Mrs. Willhelm said, rolling over on her back. "Now, go to sleep."

Angus didn't say a word.

"Angus?" Mrs. Willhelm asked. "Are you still there?" She turned to face him.

"Angus," she said, "what really happened to the cat?"

A week later, Angus had eaten all the food in the apartment. He'd even eaten all the ranch dressing and the leftover tins of cat food (the lamb variety was surprisingly delicious!). He'd eaten while the landlord banged on the door for his rent check. He'd eaten while the phone rang, and then stopped ringing. He'd eaten while he'd heard that terrible yet tasty Perry and her mother knocking on the door, calling for him and his mom.

He'd eaten through the police ringing the doorbell

and sliding a notice under the door for Angus to report to school.

But a week after that, Angus was dizzy with hunger. He'd eaten everything in the house. (Narrator note: And I mean EVERYTHING.)

He didn't even have the strength to play his banjo. So he ate that as well.

He didn't have the heart to eat his television set (and he couldn't very well stand up on his own two feet to get to it, anyway).

The phone was no longer working.

The remote was out of battery power.

Then one morning, the most amazing thing happened: Angus woke up to find a huge Christmas ham in his lap. It was large and pink and succulent. And it smelled of piggy.

Angus was so happy—he didn't question his good luck as he sank his teeth in!

A few days after Angus's last meal, the police finally had the landlord open the door.

Two of the three threw up. The third merely fainted.

The End

GREED

Picture Dick Cheney as a kid, Herman Cain as a kid, Rupert Murdoch as a kid. Now combine them—and you have little Rodney Bartholomew (pronounced "BART-olom-ewe"). Little Rodney loved one thing: money. What did he love more than money? Quick money. He was slick as an oil spill, as fast-talking as a horse-race caller, wore ascots like the Duke of York, and carried embossed business cards and a sterling silver Tiffany money clip. Little Rodney (he was quite small) was in the seventh grade at Mark Frost Academy and lived with Grandma Bartholomew in a sunny two-bedroom condo in Encino.

His bedroom walls were covered with downloaded photos and articles about his favorite modern robber barons—one entire wall was plastered with pictures of Sumner Redstone—and while his IQ was upwards of 170, he was too consumed with making fast money to spend time on his schoolwork. Why should he care about school when school didn't pay him?

Grandma Bartholomew had her speckled hands full, as she explained to me one day over a cup of peppermint tea. I'd been tutoring Rodney in math, which was the only subject he took any interest in, as long as I explained integers and negative numbers in money terms.

"I've no idea what to do with that boy," Grandma said. "He's going to end up in jail or as Bristol Palin's running mate."

Where were Dad and Mom? I looked them up on the Internet. Harry and Jillian Bartholomew were once famous for their Hair Today, Hair Tomorrow! Miracle Hair Grow System!™ Perhaps you saw their infomercials? Harry was just that—hairy! And his wife, Jillian, an ex-Playmate, was just plain silly. They died when Harry's light plane crashed into the Pacific Ocean. According to

Grandma, they were on their way to Mexico to escape something called "the IRS."

Little Rodney was skinny and wan and spent hours on his computer searching for ideas on get-rich-quick schemes. He wasn't interested in eating, unless you could drink dinner through a straw. Everything he did had to be quick. He conceived his first Ponzi scheme when he was barely out of diapers. His last matrix scam cost his fifth-grade teacher her Honda. Grandma Bartholomew had even caught him trying to hack into her bank accounts.

"I wouldn't trust that boy with a dime," Grandma warned me. "And don't you, either."

One day after school, I came over to find Rodney sulking at his desk in his bedroom, staring at an old photograph of Paul Allen, his little feet swinging, barely skimming the floor.

"He's a handsome one, that one," Rodney said in his vague British/Madonna accent.

"What's wrong?" I asked. "Rodney, where's your computer?"

"Grandmother took it away," Rodney said in another

stilted attempt at sophistication. "I'm not currently speaking to her."

I walked out of his bedroom and found Grandma sitting at her kitchen table, enjoying a game of gin with several of the "girls" in the condo retirement community.

"I had to cut off little Rodney's Internet privileges," Grandma admitted, slapping a card down on the table. The other ladies clucked their tongues, shook their white bobble heads, their eyes on their cards. They kept their distance from Rodney after he'd fleeced them in dominoes.

"What'd he do," I asked, "if I may inquire?"

"The boy stole one of my credit cards," Grandma said.

The clucking started to build.

"He tried to buy a yacht in the marina," she continued, "to rent out for sunset margarita parties."

"Grandmother, you old hen!" I heard Rodney yell from his room. "You can make a load of money doing Sunset Margarita parties!"

"He's failing every one of his classes," Grandma said,

"and now he refuses to wear his school uniform unless it's hand-stitched. He wants a bespoke uniform! I'm at the end of my rope, Perry. And what's with the accent? My people have never set foot in England."

"It's the Billionaire Boys Club syndrome. I've seen it before," I said to the old lady. "Let me see what I can do."

After all, I wanted to tell her, I've dealt with Lust, Wrath, and Gluttony—surely Greed would have a happier ending. At this point, I was losing my clientele at a rapid pace. I needed to do something, quick.

I went back into his bedroom and tried to get Rodney to start his history homework. I perused his textbook until I found something interesting. "Rodney, look at chapter three—it's all about the pharaohs," I pointed out. "All they cared about was gold and power . . . sound familiar?"

"You know I love the pharaohs. But I need current investors," Rodney said. "I'm working on a start-up."

"You have to graduate high school first, Rodney," I said.

"Why? Bill Gates didn't graduate."

"That's not true," I said, not entirely sure.

"Do you think I should get a Phantom or a Bentley when I'm sixteen?"

"What's a Phantom?"

"A car, Perry," he sneered. "Sometimes you're just so . . . common. Where do you think I should hide my offshore accounts? The Cayman Islands or Anguilla?"

"First of all, I don't think we should be having this conversation. We should be studying, not hiding assets we don't have. Secondly, how do you presume to buy a car, any car, when you don't have any money?"

"My grandmother is a very wealthy woman, Perry. Don't let this condo business fool you. That old woman's tight as a drum," Rodney said. "She's already spent my father's trust. You do know of the Bartholomews of Pink Sands, Bahamas, I presume?"

"No, Rodney, I do not," I said. "Your grandmother had to pay off all of your father's debt. She's living on a fixed income. Everything goes to tuition, uniforms, gin games, and peppermint tea."

"I remember when my parents were alive," Rodney reminisced, a dreamy look crossing his pinched face. He looked like a middle-aged banker waxing eloquent about the bailout. "We had an Italianate mansion at the top of Doheny, servants who'd beg me not to tell on them when they'd discipline me, dogs I couldn't play with because they'd bite me. My parents would leave me for weeks . . . God, they were rich and neglectful. It was heaven!"

I thought it sounded horrible. I managed to get Rodney to pay attention to his textbooks for a scant ten minutes (bribing him with a twenty-dollar bill, half my hourly rate) before I had to go to my next appointment.

Grandma, with some effort, got up from her card game and walked me to the door as I was leaving. She had lately taken to using a cane, and I noticed she was more stooped than normal. Her dowager's hump had grown, like she was hiding a kitten underneath her sweater. Her eyes were becoming foggy behind her bifocals.

"Are you okay, Grandma Bartholomew?" I asked.

She coughed from deep inside. "Growing old's not for sissies, my dear Perry," she said. "I wouldn't recommend it, but I'm not ready for the alternative, not yet."

Then she grabbed my arm, her bony fingers digging

into my skin. "Don't be surprised if something happens to me, Perry. Something . . ." She looked off in the direction of Rodney's room and wheezed. "Don't be surprised," she murmured. "I see how he eyes me. Perry, I'm raising a sociopath."

"Grandma Bartholomew," I said, "Rodney's just a kid. He's smart, and I know he's got a good heart—we just have to . . . find it."

I was crossing my fingers; I didn't know what Rodney was capable of.

I hurried home and looked up *sociopath*. Although there wasn't a photograph in the description, there might as well have been. And it would have been a photo of Rodney Bartholomew, age thirteen. No capacity for empathy? Disregard for social norms and rules?

Hi, Rodney!

I discussed the matter with my mother, the very wise and formidable (even at four feet, ten inches) Yelena Maria Gonzales. I was serving her favorite, arroz con pollo, for our dinner as she soaked her swollen feet in hot water and Epsom salt after a long day at work. It was ten o'clock at night.

"What the boy needs is gratitude. Take him to a homeless shelter," she suggested in her native Spanish.

Two days later, I tricked Rodney into going to the local homeless shelter in Sun Valley. I told him we were going to a Rich Dad Poor Dad seminar.

Instead, we met people who'd lost their jobs and their homes. We met families with small children whose next stop was living in a van. We sat with a bent, soft-spoken man who'd been an accountant with the same company for twenty-five years, whose pension plan was drained by a Bernie Madoff associate. He'd lost his wife, his family, everything.

Rodney's eyes lit up.

"*The* Bernie Madoff?" he asked the accountant. "Did you ever meet him? What was he like? I'd really like to visit him; I write him at least one letter a week."

The accountant's weary face took on a puzzled look.

"He's, like, my personal hero," Rodney explained. "I think of him as a mentor, if you will."

I dragged Rodney out by his ear—as I said, he weighs about ninety pounds.

"What do you think you're doing?" I hissed. "This is

not a joke—that man worked for twenty-five years and was left with nothing."

Rodney's face screwed up, as though he were chewing on a lemon; he was not impressed by the accountant's story.

"He should have worked smart," Rodney said. "He had twenty-five years to figure out the system. Sucker."

I felt like I'd been slapped. At that moment, I decided to quit tutoring Rodney—he was a lost cause. I couldn't waste any more precious energy on him.

"I'm sorry, Grandma," I told the old lady that afternoon. "I'm just not getting anywhere with Rodney. I tried, I really did, but I don't want to keep taking your money."

"I understand, child," she said with a sigh. "I'm at the end of my rope, myself, but he is my only grandchild . . ."

Grandma Bartholomew gave me a dry kiss on the forehead and pressed an extra, crumpled twenty-dollar bill into my hand. I looked back at her ghostly figure in the picture window as I walked toward my bus stop. I fought to keep tears from my eyes. The guilt lodged in my throat threatened to choke me.

That night, Mama listened thoughtfully, her eyes closed, as I told her about the visit to the homeless shelter, about the accountant's story, about why I had quit.

"I am not a quitter, Mama, you know this."

"You did your best, *mami*. You couldn't keep taking Grandma's money." She sighed. "That wouldn't be right."

"I'm worried about Grandma," I said. "You know, Mama, I'm even worried about Rodney."

Less than a year later, I got a phone call from a Superior Court caseworker. Rodney had just turned fourteen and was filing for emancipation from his grandmother. He claimed abuse and siphoning of his trust fund. Grandma Bartholomew was fighting the emancipation. I knew that despite everything, she, too, was worried about Rodney.

Several months went by. I got another call. This time from a man claiming to be Grandma's attorney.

"Rodney is trying to have Mrs. Bartholomew found incompetent. He's filed a 1090."

My heart froze. "That's not going to happen, right? How is Grandma?"

"She's fine. She's upset, of course. She's been in and out of the hospital with her high blood pressure."

I had to go visit her, and I had to try to talk some sense into Rodney. I took a bus after school and an hour later found myself standing in front of Grandma's door. I knocked. No one answered. I pressed my ear to the door. I didn't hear a sound. No music. No bridge game. No old voices hollering above an imaginary din. Nothing.

I rapped on the door again. Finally, I heard someone unlocking the door. Lock after lock; the process took what felt like an hour.

The door opened, barely an inch. I couldn't see anyone.

"Grandma?" I said. "It's me, Perry. Perry Gonzales."

There was no light on in the apartment. All I saw was darkness.

"Grandma?" I said. "Are you okay?"

"Are you alone?" she whispered.

"Yes," I said, fear crawling up my spine.

"No one followed you?" she asked.

"No," I said, turning around instinctively. *Am I sure? What is she talking about?*

"Come in, come in," she said, opening the door just a few inches more. "Quickly!"

I hustled in and tried to navigate the living room, but the drapes were closed. I stood in the darkness while my eyes adjusted.

Grandma was more stooped and shriveled then ever—she was disappearing before me.

"Grandma, I got a phone call—your attorney . . . he said Rodney was trying to find you incompetent," I said. "I wanted to check on you. Do you need help?"

"Oh, child. I don't think you can help. It's Rodney," she said. "He's in trouble. He borrowed money from some bad people—he invested it in some scheme, lost it all. Now he's trying to have me declared incompetent so he can get my pension, my social security, my accounts, everything I have. Perry, he wants to put me in a state-run home."

She looked so broken and small.

"They can't do that, Grandma," I said. "They'd have to prove that you're not capable of taking care of yourself."

"Rodney lies, Perry," she said. "You know that. And he's good at it. He can pass any lie detector test—he's like a reptile; his blood runs cold. Perry, he's forged documents, too—"

"Where is he?" I said. "Maybe if I talk to him . . ."

"He's in hiding," Grandma said. "I know where, but I can't tell you. He can't come home. Those people, they're Armenian Mafia. They'll kill him. The boy took their money; I told him not to. He told me they were suckers."

I left soon after, my heart heavy as I waited at the bus stop. I found myself watching my back and carefully checking out the other riders. When I got home, I ran to my mother, who was in the bedroom changing from work. I told her the story and asked her if there was anything I could do. She took off her earrings and placed them in her tiny silver jewelry box. She stared at me with her big dark eyes, our faces matching each other's in the mirror, divided only by years.

"There's nothing you can do, *mija*," she said as she shook her head. "Unless . . . Grandma Bartholomew can move in with us. You call her and let her know. She's not going to a home. We won't let that happen. We'll give her our room. We'll sleep in the living room."

I called and left Grandma Bartholomew a message on her home phone. She never returned my call.

A few days later, I left another. She never called me back.

Two weeks went by. I decided to visit again. I was worried about Grandma—she was so old and fragile. As I walked up the stairs to her place, I heard noise coming from inside.

Music.

I pressed the buzzer. I waited, then pressed it again.

There were voices coming from inside—loud voices. Happy voices.

I knocked.

Grandma Bartholomew opened the door. Sunlight flooded the stairwell. She was wearing a bright pink sweater. Her hair was silvery and reflective as a mirror and held off her face with a bejeweled hair clip. She gave me a wide smile and hugged me.

She wasn't using her cane. Her dowager's hump had shrunk.

"Perry!" she exclaimed. "How are you? Come in, dear, come in."

I walked in and saw various residents enjoying crudités and champagne cocktails. Everyone was laughing and smiling. Gone was the dark, gloomy apartment I'd been in only two weeks ago.

"Grandma, what happened? Is it your birthday?"

"No, dear," she said. "Not my birthday, but God willing, I'll have another!"

She handed me a ginger ale poured into a champagne glass.

"Where's Rodney?" I asked, looking around.

"Rodney?" she said, pursing her lips. "Rodney, ah, left us."

"He left? Is he in another school?" I asked. "Did an aunt take him?"

"Dear," Grandma Bartholomew said, "can I trust you?" She looked at me with shining eyes. I'd never seen her so happy.

"Of course," I said. If there's one thing I am, it's trustworthy. My word is bond.

"Follow me," she said. "I have something to show you."

Grandma took my hand, and I followed her into Rodney's bedroom, which was now empty of all his posters and photographs. His computer was gone. The room was filled with moving boxes, the words *Salvation Army: Save for Pickup* or *Goodwill* on them.

"Dear, Rodney is gone," she said, staring into my eyes. "You of all people will understand . . ."

She turned and rifled through papers on his desk and put her bifocals on the tip of her nose as she picked up several sheets.

"Here," she said. "Read this."

It was a life insurance policy with Grandma Bartholomew's given name on it—Helena Marjean Bartholomew—her address, and her date of birth.

It named Rodney as the beneficiary.

The policy was for $1,000,000.

(Yes, that says one million dollars.)

It was signed by Grandma.

My hands were shaking as I read the papers.

"I never took out this life insurance policy," Grandma said. "You know what this means, don't you, Perry?"

Grandma's tone changed. She no longer sounded like the sweet Grandma I knew and loved and shared tea with. She sounded resolute, cold, a businesswoman.

"He was going to . . ."

I didn't finish my sentence.

"My grandson was going to kill me," she said. "I found a bottle of rat poison in his room, behind his bookshelf. Don't ask me how I found it. I was lucky. He'd moved back in, told me everything was fine. That he had made his peace with the Armenians. I believed him."

She sighed.

"And then I found the rat poison. And you know rat

poison looks like sugar, Perry," Grandma said. "And you know I like sugar in my tea."

"Where's Rodney, Grandma?" I asked, my voice cracking. My throat was dry and my teeth started chattering.

"Do you know what rat poison does to a person's body?" Grandma asked. "It burns holes in your intestines. You die by choking on your own blood."

"Grandma . . . what happened to Rodney?" My voice fell to a whisper. My palms started to sweat. I wrapped my arms around my shoulders to keep from shivering.

"Oh, they'll find him someday, I expect," Grandma Bartholomew said. "Here and there. The Armenians are smart and helpful people, and they respect their elders, but Lord knows you can't outrun DNA."

My hand went to my mouth, holding in a scream.

Grandma chuckled to herself. "How's this for irony, Perry? The morning after I called those boys, I had a doctor's appointment. As it turns out, my days are numbered. Without treatment, the doctors have given me just six months."

"Oh, no, Grandma," I said. "You have to get treatment. You have to! We can figure all this out. My mother and I, we'll help you—"

"No, child." The old lady patted my hand. "I'm happy. Every single day of those six months is going to be joyful. Every day will be filled with sunlight and friends and peppermint tea and the music of my youth. And when it's all over, I'm going out with a smile on this old face. I'm at peace."

She looked at me, as though surprised I was still there.

"Would you like something to eat, dear? Are you hungry? There's plenty of food." She gave me a big smile.

"I'm good, Grandma," I managed to say. "If it's all the same to you, I think I'll be going."

"Okay, child," she said. "Oh. Remember our agreement, now."

She waggled her finger at me. I nodded. The music changed to a new song.

"Ooh, that's my song," Grandma said, clapping her hands and humming a few bars. "I'd better join my guests. Don't want to be a bad hostess!"

She hopped up from the bed and headed to the doorway, then turned.

"Grandma had a few tricks up her antique lace sleeves, eh, Perry?" she said. "Sometimes, my dear, justice has to be served in a banana smoothie through a straw. Oh, and sweetie, just take anything you want from these boxes. It's all going to Goodwill."

I stood on shaky legs and watched her rush to mingle with her friends. I looked around the room, which had expanded without the Forbes Fortune 500 faces bearing down on me.

My eyes fell on a knit cap that would have suited me perfectly. A deep maroon. I knew it was cashmere. I thought about how good it would feel on cold mornings at the bus stop.

I decided against taking it. It would have been greedy.

The End

Recently, I had to get a cell phone. I was initially against the idea, because I don't want anything getting in the way of my five-, ten-, fifteen-, and twenty-five-year plans. (Bennington College . . . bestselling author . . . Harvard Law . . . Supreme Court bench.) Cell phones are a distraction: Cell phones mean texting, cell phones mean music, cell phones mean apps—which mean playing games.

Esteemed Admissions Committee, you know me, Perry Gonzales, pretty well by now. Do you think I want to waste my life playing computer games? I've seen it happen before. I've seen what games can do.

Games kill.

My mother, the upstanding Yelena Maria Gonzales, insisted that I buy my own phone when her voice mail crashed after so many Mark Frost Academy parents left messages asking for my services. They offered money, apartments, vacations, sports cars (I'm fourteen years old). As you know, I'm a highly regarded tutor at Mark Frost Academy. I'm not being cocky—my reputation precedes me, as they say. I've been known to rescue even the dullest kids from the doldrums D's and the far-from-fantastic F's. I have a knack, a gift, if you will.

One of the parents who called me was Sheldon Turkle (pronounced "Turk-LAY") the head honcho of Completely WorldWide Studios. To be more precise, his office got in touch with me. His assistant, Bethanny, called, then put me on hold for five minutes, then called me again and forgot what she was calling about. She sounded like she was crying. In the background, I heard a lot of yelling and swear words, the specifics of which I won't share with you.

Between her tears, Bethanny begged me to go to the Turkle household that very afternoon. I told her I was busy, which is true. I have school, I'm the goalie for the Mark Frost Academy ninth-grade girls soccer team, I play clarinet in the school band, and I work five days a week. I couldn't possibly tutor any more hours.

Bethanny said Mr. Turkle would put me in a movie if I tutored his son, Timmy.

I have no interest in being an actress, I told her. I'm a writer.

She said Mr. Turkle would buy my first script.

I told her I wanted to be a journalist. Or a novelist.

She told me he would buy my opening line.

We'll see, I said. She didn't sound too happy.

A few days later, I called her back. I was feeling guilty, and as it turned out, one of my clients had gone into juice rehab (he's fifteen and addicted to juicing). I had an opening that afternoon at four. Take it or leave it. Unfortunately for me, but fortunately for the purposes of this story and my future career as a Pulitzer Prize–winning journalist/PEN Award–winning novelist, the Turkles jumped on it.

And on that day, at precisely four p.m., in an enormous, enormously cold, ultra-modern home filled with art and sculptures and absolutely not one speck of dust, nor carpets nor pillows nor comfortable chairs, I met Sloth.

Young Turkle's parents weren't home. Dad was at work, and Mom . . . Mom was also at her job. Mirella, the El Salvadoran housekeeper/nanny, explained that Mrs. Turkle's job was something called "appointments."

Mirella escorted me downstairs in a sleek steel, spotless elevator to the underground screening room. As we rode, we exchanged pleasantries in Spanish. She seemed pleased and almost relieved that I, the tutor, was Hispanic.

The steel doors of the elevator opened and I was hit by a putrid, sickeningly sweet smell. Like body odor mixed with rotten fruit.

I covered my nose and mouth while my eyes adjusted slowly to the dark.

On a giant screen that dominated the giant cavelike room, dirty, bloodied soldiers were shooting and being shot by what appeared to be the undead.

Here we go, I thought. I was beginning to sympathize with the undead, given my recent adventures in tutoring.

A figure, a boy I took to be Timmy Turkle, was reclining on a sectional couch, the only one in the house, 3-D glasses glued to his head, hands attached to his video game controller. From what I could see, he appeared to be all limb and no torso, like an insect.

Mirella called out his name; it was impossible to hear over the din of automatic weapons fire. She shouted his name again and again and finally reached over and shook him by the shoulder. Timmy shrugged her off and continued to shoot. The undead were having a bad day.

"Maybe I should turn on the lights!" I shouted.

"Should we wait for him to finish his game?" Mirella yelled.

"No!" If I had learned one thing from my adventures, it was that the word *no* was due for a comeback.

In fact, I thought as I searched for the lights, we should have a parade for the word *no,* have an annual *No* Day. A moment of silence for *no.* *No* could save humanity. No to war, no to poverty, no to video games . . .

I flipped the light switch on (which is, incidentally, the reverse of *no*). Timmy made a high-pitched screech that sounded like a hundred nails on a chalkboard and whipped around to face us. What I could see of his expression, despite the cloak of the 3-D glasses, was fear, as though he were staring at ghosts rather than his lifelong babysitter and a short fourteen-year-old girl with dark braids. His skin was gray, and his body had no muscle tone; his skinny arms in his loose-fitting tank top looked like spaghetti (pasta, for those of you who don't remember the glory days of spaghetti).

"*Mijo*, this is Perry," Mirella said, gently touching his shoulder. "She's here to help you with your schoolwork."

Timmy didn't bother taking off his 3-D glasses as he shifted and writhed and gave up trying to get off the couch to greet me. He then struggled to raise his hand to shake mine. When our hands finally met, I was horrified to see that his thumbs were the size of large turnips—they were thick and bulbous. A metallic sound came out of his body—his version of grunting a hello. I was scared that perhaps he was unable to form a sentence. I knew he was close to twelve or thirteen, but it was hard to tell what age he was, he appeared so wan.

I looked at Timmy and thought of mushrooms. Gray mushrooms. How long had he been in here, in this cave? A shiver went down my spine. I was familiar with that shiver.

I asked Mirella, in Spanish, *"¿Cuántos años tienes?"*

"Catorce."

I knew my eyes bugged out as I raised my eyebrows. Fourteen! How was that possible? Mirella nodded, then shook her head, understanding my shock as her big brown eyes blinked back tears.

"Mijo, take off your glasses," Mirella told Timmy in a soft voice.

"Can it wait?" He could speak! Sure, he sounded odd, but my heart skipped. I was cheered by this simple skill. I'd learned to expect the worst.

"I'm playing Boris, Mirella," Timmy continued. His voice. How can I explain his voice? If it were a color, it would be the color of sky the morning after a bombing raid. Nothingness. Devoid of life.

It reminded me of an Apple computer voice. (Please don't sue me.)

"Me and Boris—we're on the sixth level of the ninth ward—I'm down three—if I stop now, I won't win. I can't stop now!"

"*Mijo . . . por favor. Para mí.*"

Timmy sighed and grunted, then attempted to slide the glasses back over his head. They were stuck. Stuck as though they would be there permanently. Stuck as though they were part of his skin, of that gray, skinny body of his.

Mirella leaned over in front of him and pulled and pulled until the glasses popped off his head, making a loud suction noise.

I gasped and covered my mouth to keep from throwing up.

Timmy's eyes were enormous, at least ten times bigger than normal human eyes; they claimed half the available landmass of his head. There were deep, purple divots in his cheeks where the glasses had been lodged for weeks, months, years? He had bald patches on his dome where the glasses had destroyed his hair follicles.

But those eyes—I had seen eyes like those before.

Timmy Turkle was a human fly.

He grunted and said hi in that same weird computer monotone. (Should I just say *computer* instead of *Apple*, Admissions Committee? I really don't want any trouble with corporate lawyers. From what I've seen at school, they're very punitive. But dapper.)

I looked at Mirella, who had tears in her eyes. I needed to leave that room.

"Would you like some water?" she asked me.

I nodded. I was speechless.

"We'll be back, *mijo*."

I tried to give Timmy a natural smile; I'm afraid I merely grimaced. He grunted, grabbed his 3-D glasses, slipped them back on over those giant fly eyes, and restarted his video game. The automated gunfire made me jump as I entered the elevator. I was a wreck, and I don't wreck easily. Surely, you know this by now.

"Mirella . . . what happened to Timmy?" I asked.

What I found out from Mirella, over a delicious and necessary cup of dulce de leche, was that Timmy had spent the past thirteen out of his fourteen years on that very couch in the screening room, playing video games. His eyes had adapted not only to living in the dark almost permanently, but to his years of exorbitant electronic viewing.

It was like Darwinian theory on speed.

Mirella started crying in earnest, her tears dropping one by one into her cup. She had begged his parents, Sheldon and Krissy, to cut Timmy off from the TV—he'd never learned to throw a ball, pet a dog, swim in the ocean. He'd never learned to tie his shoes or say his nightly prayers. Mirella thought of taking Timmy, of kidnapping him and taking him back to her native country to live amongst her large family, to live that most precious of all things everywhere—a normal life.

Timmy had lived his life in front of a screen.

The Turkles wouldn't listen—they didn't have time. They led "crazy-busy" lives. (I've learned this term from some of "my" parents—what it means is, "I make myself 'crazy' by staying 'busy' with things I don't need.")

Now, Mirella feared . . . now, it was too late.

"It's never too late," I said, perhaps naively—I am fourteen years old, after all. I have to have something to believe in before I grow up and lose all belief in anything.

Mirella grabbed my hand and held it tight.

"*Mija*," she said, her large eyes shiny and wet with tears only a mother could shed. "*Pobrecito* Timmy is in trouble. God help me, that boy will die in that room."

I couldn't help but feel it, too.

That night, I consulted my mother, the ever-so-wise Yelena Maria Gonzales, as to whether I should take on this new challenge. Timmy Turkle was failing every single class. From looking at the files I'd been provided by Mirella, I could tell that Timmy's native intelligence was high—he tested at genius level on the IQ tests, and Mensa stuffed his mailbox with mailings—but it was doubtful he'd ever actually read a book.

I mean, ever.

Like, in his entire life.

"Mama, I want to help him, but I'm not sure I can," I

told my mother as she rested her feet on the ottoman after a long day at General Hospital. "The situation seems so hopeless."

She eyed me from her chair. Many of her patients were indigent, mentally ill, or at the end of long, hard lives. She treated each one as if they were a king or prince, a queen or princess.

Yeah, she's a saint.

My mother took a deep breath, which I knew meant that she disagreed with my assessment, but also that she was thinking of the right words to choose.

After a long pause, she said, "*Mija*, you must meet with his parents. Then we can make a decision."

Beat. There was more.

"A thing is hopeless only if you decide it is so."

<hr/>

Securing a meeting with the Turkles proved to be rather, um, difficult. Both parents had several assistants, and the assistants all seemed to be fighting with one another.

There were a lot of tears, a lot of yelling, and a lot of *I'm not speaking to hers.*

It was a dysfunctional family pyramid.

It took several weeks of cajoling and providing support staff therapy before I finally found myself sitting (in an uncomfortable yet aesthetically pleasing chair) across from Krissy and Sheldon Turkle at a long, granite table overlooking their sparkling, untouched swimming pool.

Mirella had told me that Timmy was, of course, downstairs in the screening room/hole.

"Shoot, Perry." Mr. Turkle's voice emerged like a cannon shot.

"Well, Mr. Turkle, I wanted to meet with you about tutoring your son—"

"Do you know anything about art?" he demanded.

"Me? Ah, not really."

"Timmy was such a sweet baby. Mirella, remember when you used to sleep with him?" Mrs. Turkle asked as Mirella poured orange juice.

"I'm thinking about buying this piece, but this ass— 'scuse me—jerkoff keeps jerking me around," Mr. Turkle grumbled.

"Mr. Turkle, I'm concerned that Timmy's issues may be too far along—" I said.

Mr. Turkle's BlackBerry buzzed and his iPhone vibrated. I lost him as he tapped ferociously at the Black-Berry keys; his iPhone vibrated off the side of the table and dropped to the ground.

He took out another one.

"Screw that guy!" he yelled into his second iPhone.

I turned to his wife. "Mrs. Turkle, according to Timmy's testing, his IQ is quite high—so there is some hope—"

Mrs. Turkle, who heretofore had been staring at me with bright blue blank eyes, her eyebrows in a constant state of surprise in a face that looked cemented into place, suddenly started talking.

"No, no, they can't be seated next to each other. Stacy married Kacy's third husband, remember?"

I realized that under her bushel of blond hair, a Blue-tooth was attached to her ear. I sighed.

Her eyes widened at me.

"Sorry, honey, you were saying?"

"Have you tried to get Timmy to stop playing video games?"

Mrs. Turkle got a faraway look in her eyes as Mr. Turkle continued to tap on his BlackBerry keys and grumble.

"Of course. When he was two, we tried bribing him with his favorite foods. Twizzlers, Sour Patch Kids, that sort of thing. Then we tried discipline. Like, if he didn't go to bed on time, he would only be able to play video games for three hours, not four. But it's so hard to follow through, don't you agree? Being a mother is just so exhausting. Oops!"

I lost her as she took another phone call.

Mirella looked at me and shrugged her shoulders as she picked up plates. The Turkles had eaten nothing.

"One time, the parents, they cut off the electric," Mirella said to me in the kitchen as she put plates and cups in the dishwasher after our "meeting." I put my backpack down and started helping her.

"I remember: It was just me and the boy, he was eight—they were on vacation. I told them to do it. It's the last time I've seen him smile."

Mr. Turkle swept through the kitchen and narrowed his eyes at me, as if wondering why I was still there.

"If this is a shakedown," he said, stopping in his tracks, "I'll just pay you double, how's that?"

"A what?" I asked.

"Isn't she sweet, Sheldon?" Mrs. Turkle walked in on five-inch sneakers, the latest unattractive, nonsensical trend on the Westside that everyone had to have. "Are you bilingual, sweetheart?"

Mr. Turkle suddenly banged his BlackBerry on the kitchen island.

"You're good! What are you, a pro? I'll pay triple! What are you doing with my kid again?"

I looked to Mirella for support and clarification, but her back was to me as she wiped down the kitchen countertop.

I knew what my mother would say. I needed to clear my schedule. The situation here was dire.

"I'll be back this afternoon," I said. "We'll work three days a week. No need to pay me double or triple."

I left, moving as fast as I could without knocking anything over.

"What's your game?" I heard Mr. Turkle yell after me.

I approached Timmy very carefully during our sessions. I knew I would have to draw him out of his cave before being able to teach him. And if it worked—if he got C's instead of F's—I would consider our time together victorious.

In fact, I thought on that first day, if I could get those glasses off his head long enough for him to take a shower, it would be my greatest victory yet.

I failed miserably. On all accounts.

I could barely get Timmy to acknowledge my presence, much less open a book, take pen to paper, write an essay, decode an equation. Timmy wasn't rude, he was just completely and utterly disconnected from the real world.

After a couple weeks, it was clear that I was in over my head.

I consulted on the case with my mother. We were shopping at the corner market painted bright green with pink letters, the colors of guava, on a bustling Saturday morning, moving languorously among the mangoes and papayas, the dragon fruit and the prickly pears. It was my mother's rare day off, and she loved to stop and listen and touch and smell and linger in the aromas that brought back her childhood.

I hated to interrupt her meditation as I walked in her steps, shadowing her gestures and silent greetings. The local grocer, a stocky bald man with big, helpful hands that he rubbed nervously on his apron, had a schoolboy crush on my mother. This much a blind man could see, a deaf man could hear. He would slice open a piece of fruit at the slightest nod, or offer a taste of his slow-cooked carne asada. He noticed me, her shadow, with a blank, lost smile, his eyes only for Yelena Maria Gonzales. I was cute, sure, but my mother was, like, made of movie-star materials.

And right when I was about to bring up the question of Timmy, my mother gave me the answer.

"You need to work differently, *mija*," she said as she held a ripe guava to her nose, and then to mine. "He is not a bad boy. He is like this fruit—a bit spoiled, but salvageable."

"I can't. All he wants to do is play video games," I whined. "I can't compete against Grand Theft Killing Machine. I'm only a kid. An amazing kid, but still . . ."

I was joking. You know, sort of.

"So play with him," she said. "Start there."

She ran her hand across the rainbow lining the grocer's pallets. Sometimes, I think color must have been invented in Mexico.

"If you're an amazing kid, *mija*, your mom must be *muy especial*." She winked at me as the grocer covered her in his puppy-eyed gaze.

"Timmy," I said, "I'm going to make you a bet. If I beat you in the game of your choice . . . okay, the easiest game of your choice, you have to allow me to tutor you for three weeks."

Timmy looked at me and smiled slightly, showing small gray teeth.

Ooh, signs of a positive emotion . . .

"Okay," he said. "And if I win?"

"I leave you alone. Deal?" I held out my hand, covering my grimace as he shook it. I'd forgotten about that disfigured thumb.

"Deal," he said flatly. The hint of the smile was gone. I'd lost him already.

I lost the game, of course. I know that would have made a good story—but really, did you think I had a chance? I didn't know my A button from my B, my X from my Y.

I held the controller upside down for the first three minutes.

But a funny thing happened. Timmy saw that I was determined to be a fixture on his couch, and he seemed resigned to my company. And seeing how hopeless my game was, he sparked to teaching me how to play. Like stepping foot onto foreign soil, I had to learn the language first—the language of video games. He taught me terms like *deathmatch* (killing game), *frag* (a kill), *headshot* (a kill to the head), and *MMO* (see *deathmatch*).

Timmy called me a "noob" when I asked him how to survive an alien onslaught in Halo. He mocked me when my avatar was blown to bits by faceless commandos.

Slowly, slowly, I worked his schoolwork in, between games . . .

What were his favorite games? I don't want to encourage video game use, but okay, Timmy's top five favorites, in no particular order: Halo 2, Star Wars, Madden NFL 12, Grand Theft Auto and GTA3, and Golf.

If you play these games, you may be familiar with Timmy's personal signature—he was usually in the top three of all the players in the entire world, including

Japan and Korea, where several gamers have died after playing for days in a row. For example, on Halo 2, he's listed as TURK1—with 5,687,002 points at the time we played together.

I learned that Timmy had a running feud that had stretched on for years with a boy named Boris Blankeleva, who lived halfway across the world in Moscow. He showed me Boris's profile. Boris was a big boy with a big appetite—fifteen years old, but about six feet, six inches, three hundred pounds. He lived with an older sister, an ex–Miss Universe who worked at a nightclub as a "hostess," and a grandfather who drank vodka for breakfast and slept all day. He was very, very good at video games. Which meant he was very, very bad at most other things. Like school. Like personal hygiene.

Just like Timmy.

<hr />

By the end of the school year, Timmy had brought his grade point average from a 1.3 to a 3.2. He'd even made up his work for grades three, five, six, and seven. Plus, using a bottle of AXE shower gel, I was able to cajole him into taking daily five-minute showers; he loved smelling like a masculine floral arrangement. His favorite was Anarchy Revitalizing Shower Gel—Snake Peel Shower Scrub was a close second.

But best of all, and my proudest achievement to date: Timmy shut down the video game system long enough to read a book. *The Catcher in the Rye*. I can't think about him asking me what game Holden Caulfield would be playing today without getting choked up.

We celebrated with one final game of Halo.

I lost, of course. Let's not get crazy here.

June was just around the corner. This would be a great summer for Timmy. For the first time in his life, he was going away to summer camp. For six whole weeks! Open Sky Camp allowed no cell phones, no televisions, no personal gaming devices, no electronics of any kind. Timmy would be hiking, mountain biking, water-skiing, roasting marshmallows, interacting with actual human kids, and communing with something called "the great outdoors."

Somehow, Timmy had agreed to it. Mirella was going to take time to visit her parents in El Salvador, who hadn't seen her in years. The Turkles were going on a cruise of the Greek islands and would be completely unreachable.

And me? I had a full summer ahead—lots of kids to tutor, tons of books to read. Maybe I'd take a weekend here and there to drive with my mom to Santa Barbara; we liked to camp out on the coast.

My summer would be just the way I like it: uneventful.

—⋆—⋆—

I received a call from Mirella in August.

"Timmy never made it to camp!" she said in Spanish, her words so hurried, it was hard to understand what she was saying.

"What? What do you mean?"

"I got off the plane and drove out two hours this morning," she said. "The counselors said he just never showed up! They tried to reach his parents, they tried to reach me—this is all my fault!"

"Have you been to the house?"

"I'm afraid, miss. I'm afraid to go."

"I'll meet you there," I said. I didn't want Mirella going in there alone. I was trying to keep my hopes up, but I was afraid of what she might find. My mom was already at work at the hospital, so I took the bus. An hour later, I was standing in front of the Turkle mansion with Mirella at my side, holding on to me.

"It's going to be okay," I reassured her, patting her hand.

She explained that the house had been completely closed down for the whole summer. No one had been inside—the only people there had been the gardeners, who worked on the expansive lawn and hillside. Mirella had already spoken with them; they'd seen nothing. No one had wandered outside the house for weeks. And as far as they could tell, no one was inside, either.

We walked into the foyer. There was a sweet, sickly smell in the air that hit me the moment we opened the door. Mirella took a step back. I held out my hand for her, and we walked through to the kitchen together.

The refrigerator was open. Coke cans were littered everywhere. The trash was overflowing. The sink was full. Empty food containers crowded the tabletops.

"I think we should go downstairs," I said.

Mirella just nodded, her eyes wide with fear.

We took the elevator down. The steel doors opened.

The room was dark.

A familiar smell hit my nose. Timmy was here—but where?

The big screen flickered ominously. The same music loop played over and over again. I felt like I was trapped in a horror film. I shook off my fear and stepped inside.

On the screen, underneath the Halo logo, were listed two names: TURK1 in first place with 6,300,203 points; BorisBeast in second with 6,300,201 points.

I couldn't see Timmy's silhouette against the screen. The room was empty.

"Timmy?" I called out.

"¿Mijito?" Mirella called.

I turned on the lights. Timmy was nowhere to be found.

"The pool!" Mirella shouted, and bolted toward the elevator. Timmy had never learned to swim.

I stayed where I was, then walked toward the couch and stood over it. I picked up the controller, which was on the floor, as though it had just been dropped and forgotten. Timmy's 3-D glasses lay next to a pile of clothes. The clothes, Timmy's favorite tank top and basketball shorts, were covered in layers of fine, gray dust. I picked up the tank top and a cloud of dust blew up in my face. I choked and hacked and waved at the air.

When the air cleared, I noticed something on the 3-D glasses. I picked them up and held them up as the screen flickered in the background.

A tuft of hair was attached to the hinge.

I don't remember much after that. Mirella told me she had heard a scream and a thud and had come rushing back downstairs brandishing a kitchen knife.

I had fainted and bumped my head on the coffee table.

The Turkles preferred to believe that Timmy had escaped to Moscow, where he could meet up with Boris and continue his gaming unabated. They insisted that Mirella vacuum up the mess downstairs.

Mirella and I, and my mother?

We went to church the following Sunday after carefully placing the contents of the vacuum bag in an urn. The priest performed a small ceremony for the three of us.

"*Cenizas a las cenizas,*" he said, "*polvo al polvo.*"

Ashes to ashes, dust to dust.

The End

ENVY

veces," I said to my mother in her native tongue, "I wish we lived in a house. An actual house. Like, a big house. Where I could have my own room. And a pool—a lap pool so I could do . . . laps. But I know laps aren't going to happen, so why can't I spend *my* money that *I* earned on a new purse . . . or a pair of cool shoes? I don't have one pair of cool shoes!"

My mother and I were experiencing an occurrence that is rare as a red moon: We were having an argument. I wanted to spend some of the money I make babysitting and tutoring on something frivolous—so maybe, for once, I could be like all the other kids at Mark Frost Academy. I hate standing out, with my black hair that's never even been layered and my clarinet case and my white tube socks; the one piece of jewelry I wear is a tiny gold cross, given to me when I was a baby.

After all, I've been doing great with my tutoring business. Luckily for me, there are, well, a plethora of idiots at my school. (It's not that the kids are dumb; it's worse, much worse. They're *entitled*.)

My mother just watched me with her wise, peaceful brown eyes. She was calm. *Too* calm. Nothing I could say or do, no insult I halfheartedly hurled, would shake her resolve. The more I pleaded, the more I knew I was fighting an uphill battle.

"Beware of envy, *mija*." My mother put her soft, warm hand against my cheek. "Envy is poison for the soul." She leaned forward, her dark almond eyes steady. "Envy may be the most dangerous sin of all."

I shuddered. Envy? Everybody gets envious—what's the big deal? I was too angry to agree with her. Wrath was my go-to sin that night. But a few months after our argument, I thought back on that moment and her prophetic words.

Why is my mother always . . . *correcto*?

<hr />

Model-tall, model-thin Ekaterina Schadenfreude (pronounced "SHAY-den-FROID"), thirteen going on fourteen, was a beautiful girl with a major problem: She wanted what everyone else had. Period. And she was always mad that other kids, especially other girls, got everything they wanted and didn't deserve (in her humble opinion). Like boyfriend jeans and ponchos, front-row seats to a Jason Mraz concert, the latest Nicole Richie cropped bob, the cutest boy in the eighth grade.

She rode a roller coaster of emotions (like a Mariah Carey song); Ekaterina found pleasure in others' misfortune (schadenfreude) and pain in others' good fortune (envy). Envy is basically schadenfreude's sourpuss sister.

Let's put it this way: Whether Ekaterina was *happy*

that her current best friend Isabel flunked her math test or her ex–best friend Ennui's boyfriend dumped her or *unhappy* because her ex-ex–best friend Olivia's science project was picked by the National Science Committee or her ex-ex-ex–best friend Thalia's horse just got five blue ribbons at a recent horse show, the girl was not a lot of fun to be around.

I was called to Ekaterina's estate, Villa Von Konigsbergen, by her ex-supermodel mother, Elisabetta Konigsbergen-Schadenfreude. I was frightened as I approached the house—it had sprung from a Gothic fairy tale, with turrets and gabled roofs and gargoyles, surrounded by eerie ebony statues that seemed to change shape as I walked gingerly past. There was no doorbell and no intercom on the giant arched wooden front door. Just your average medieval-looking lion's head iron door knocker.

A tall, colorless butler opened the door and escorted me past the foyer into the sitting room without uttering a word. I wish I could say things were lightening up, but the house's interior made the exterior look like a ride at Disneyland.

The sitting room was dark and gloomy, with over-size fixtures and an inky, frayed velvet couch that looked like it was smuggled out of the Rhineland a hundred years ago. I tried turning on an old Tiffany lamp, but it wouldn't work. There were paintings, large gray-hued industrial pieces, but the dominating decorative feature was dozens of silver-framed photographs of Ekaterina's mother posing with various heads of state and famous actors. Many of the photos appeared to be cropped.

As I waited in the sitting room, serenaded by the grandfather clock and the sound of my own breathing (while questioning my sanity), a pack of Doberman pinschers charged in, growling and snapping as I jumped onto a chair, using my Hello Kitty backpack to shield myself. I yelled for the butler, for Ms. Konigsbergen-Schadenfreude (which was even harder to pronounce in my panicked state)—anyone!

Ms. Konigsbergen-Schadenfreude swooped in, making a grand entrance in a beaded evening gown. She yelled at the dogs in guttural German, and they instant-ly retreated, transforming into whimpering, toe-licking Chihuahuas.

This is what I knew about Ekaterina and her family: Ekaterina's parents had been divorced for six years and in court ever since. Ms. Konigsbergen-Schadenfreude viewed divorce court as some would view a gym—a good place to burn calories. Once an internationally acclaimed beauty, Ms. K-S (May I? You get it, right?) had appeared on the cover of German *Vogue* over two hundred times—a world record, even more times than Claudia Schiffer, whose name Ms. K-S could not say without spitting.

If Ekaterina's mother weren't over six feet tall and all shoulders, it would be difficult to recognize her week to week. She was constantly changing her hairstyle, makeup, wardrobe, boyfriends, cars, even her face. Her cheekbones used to appear merely superhuman (she is a German supermodel, after all), but now they looked like she was harboring a family of chipmunks. Her lips expanded and retracted with the Santa Anas.

Ms. K-S insisted we move to the dining room, where we could enjoy an afternoon sauerkraut and Wiener schnitzel (she made her own sausage, she told me proudly). Ekaterina's mom was about three times taller than me (in spiked heels); I dutifully followed, as did the dogs.

I was seated in a giant baroque chair, which threatened to swallow me whole, and tried to ignore the dogs slavering at their mistress's side, eyeing me like a breakfast burrito.

Ekaterina's mother demanded, in her Germanaccented English, that I help her daughter. Her grades had fallen and could not get up. It was all I could do to concentrate on her words and not the pool floats where her mouth should be.

I thought back on my experiences with Ekaterina. I'd first noticed her in biology class—she was hard to miss, almost as tall as her mother, but blonder and as stunning as a magazine cover brought to life. Her prettiness was annoying—no airbrushing, wind machine, or sex tape necessary—this girl had the goods.

Instead of thanking her lucky stars and paying attention to her schoolwork, Ekaterina would just look around, studying other kids. I could see what Ms. Genetic Lottery Winner was thinking: *I wish I had this, I hate her, I wish I had that. Her hair is shiny. I wish I had*

I wish I had—I want those boots—I wish, wish, wish, wish,
wish . . .

She would make a face if Suzette walked in carrying
the latest Celine purse over her shoulder; she would
snicker when Edgar stuttered when the teacher called
on him . . .

I thought it must be exhausting to be her.

Once I won over the dogs (I brought liver treats for Hermann, Jasper, and Charles), my sessions with Ekaterina
would go something like this:

"Let's turn to page eighty-four in your mythology
textbook."

"Did you see what Mavis was wearing today?" Ekaterina would toss her hair, sending sparks of light up. "I
mean, that pattern was, like, so unflattering—she could
lose a few, right?"

After a few sessions with Ekaterina, I was still basically
getting nowhere—she wouldn't and couldn't stop talking

about other people. And it wasn't just her monologues about who had what and who was dating whom and who was going to St. Barts on spring vacation (I didn't even know what that was) and who was wearing the latest rag & bone (ditto). She'd ask me a million questions. Like, how'd I grow my hair so long? Did I dye it? Were my lashes real? How poor was I? Had I ever cheated on a test?

I'd just sigh and close my books after an hour, vowing to pay Ms. K-S back.

At my cozy little apartment one night, over my mom's hometown specialty—grilled red snapper with fresh lime—I asked my mother about Ekaterina's particular syndrome.

Yelena Maria Gonzales thought about it for a moment. "Ekaterina wants to be like everyone she sees," she said, "because she's forgotten who she is."

My mother, as usual, hit the nail on the *cabeza*. Ekaterina essentially had no identity, which is a sad thing for someone with such an unusual name. I'm sure you'll agree.

In the ensuing weeks, things went from bad . . . to really weird.

Ekaterina changed clothes, hairstyles, and makeup, redecorated her room, and altered her diet obsessions until the real, true, authentic Ekaterina began to disappear completely.

Whenever I arrived at her house, I wasn't sure whom I would find. When I opened the door to her room (the door changed colors weekly, the posters changed daily), I was constantly being surprised. And not in a good way.

One day a petite, Rapunzel-haired blonde named Kathee (two *e*'s) appeared, wearing a bandage dress and a pouty smile, with a total obsession for *The Real Housewives of* Wherever.

The next day, there would be a brooding brunette named Aniretake (*Ekaterina* spelled backward—it took me a while) wearing black nail polish and a nostril piercing, who eschewed all social media and would only listen to the Killers. Over and over again.

Soon, a tall redhead named Tina in a tie-dyed maxi dress wearing a peace sign around her neck appeared. On her door were various bumper stickers. Antiwar, anti–global warming, anti-anti . . . She really wanted to talk to me, a full-blooded Latina, about the repression of the native Indian people in the state of Oaxaca, Mexico.

With each transformation, Ekaterina's (or whatever her name was) voice would change, her friends would change, her least favorite classes would shift.

The blonde hated PE.

The brunette hated Algebra 2.

The redhead was calm and motivated to do well in all her courses, especially English Lit (I liked her the most and hoped she would stick around for more than a few days).

But I'm not going to lie; I was starting to get freaked out. Ekaterina's mother was sending me a check for my services each week—but I thought it was time for a meeting. My mother agreed.

"You're losing your daughter."

Ekaterina's mother sat across from me in the dining room in one of those giant baroque chairs. My feet couldn't reach the floor. Her lips were pursed. At first, I thought she was thinking. But then I realized that's how she'd had them done—to be in a constant state of pursing.

"Ekaterina is doing much better in school," she declared, expressionless.

"Yes," I said. "The redhead is, definitely. I like her. But it's taken a lot of work. This isn't just about school. Have you noticed anything . . . different about your daughter?"

"Is she doing the drugs?" She seemed concerned, but remained . . . expressionless. I'd seen this syndrome amongst the moms at Mark Frost Academy—I called them "cement heads" (never to their frozen faces!). Botox seemed to be part of their four food groups, along with Restylane, Juvéderm, and kale.

"No," I said, "I don't think that's part of the problem."

"Oh, thank God," she said. "So what is issue?"

"You don't notice? All the changes she's going through?"

She stared down at me from her perch, pursed lips and all.

"Her hair?" I ventured.

"Yessss."

"Her . . . wardrobe?" I tried.

"Yes, Ekaterina likes to change the clothes. She iss über-creative."

"Okay. Her . . . friends," I said. "What about them? They change every few weeks. That doesn't seem healthy, and her constant feuds interfere with her concentration."

"Girls. They are jealous." She sized me up. "Perhaps you would not understand. You are so lucky to be average."

I sat back, then shook my head. Ms. K-S waved me off with her large hand, saying something dismissive in German. I don't know German, but I was pretty sure the writing was on the chalkboard. I excused myself as the dogs nipped at my heels. I gave them the rest of my liver treats, certain that I would never return.

A few days later, Ekaterina's mother left a voice message on my phone to the effect that, as Ekaterina's grades had improved considerably, she would no longer be needing my services.

So much for honesty being the best policy.

Sometime in the spring, I noticed that Ekaterina hadn't been in school for a few weeks. I just assumed that, like so many other students, she'd been sent away for an extended vacation (read: Utah; read: rehab). But as I was heading to another student's home down her street, I saw flyers posted on every telephone pole and tree:

MISSING:

EKATERINA SCHADENFREUDE

REWARD!

There was a picture of Ekaterina—tall and thin, with her natural blond hair and preternaturally beautiful face.

She was almost . . . unrecognizable. The picture had been taken a year before, in her near-original state.

I was horrified and worried. I called her mother to see what had happened—and what I could do to help.

She left a message for me to meet her at the house. She was something called "post-op" and could not leave the premises.

"It was awful," Ms. K-S said in her drawing room, her face bruised and wrapped in white medical tape, rolls of gauze poking out of her nostrils. She sounded a million times older than the last time I spoke with her.

"The dogs," she said with a sigh. "They ran her off."

"What? Her own dogs?"

"Well, you know Ekaterina—she iss über-creative soul—she was constantly evolving . . ."

"Evolving."

"Well, I'm afraid my babies, they no longer recognized her."

"The dogs?"

"Yes, my children, the dogs." She sniffed. "One day Ekaterina came home from school, and they just . . ." She shook her bandaged head.

"Oh my God," I said.

"I came home and thought I saw a prowler; she must have forgotten her key and ze butler was pruning. You know, several houses have been burglarized in my neighborhood, it's terrible."

"Wait—you called the dogs on her?"

"Well, yes. I didn't know it was my Ekaterina. Jasper and Charles, they ran her off," she said. "Hermann stood watch. Poor thing, they wouldn't let her near the house. By the time I realized my mistake, it was all over. They'd taken her backpack, pieces of her very cool, latest sweater; they ate her iPhone and one very intense Louboutin." She choked back a sob.

"Oh my God, oh my God," I said. "Where'd she go?"

"No one knows. I keep putting flyers up, but I'm afraid the picture is from last year—when she ran off she had shaved her head like Miley Cyrus and dyed her stubble pink. Which was totally creative and evolved, you know? But I don't have a picture. Sad."

"This is so terrible," I said. "Poor Ekaterina . . ."

"Yes. Imagine. I couldn't recognize my own daughter. I told her all the time to be happy with who she is—like me." Ms. K-S pushed bloodied gauze back up into her nostril.

I didn't know what to say. I told her I would keep a keen eye out for Ekaterina and report back any sightings. I walked out of that dark Gothic mansion shadowed by my memories of Ekaterina and sadder than I'd ever been in my life.

Sometimes, when I'm riding the bus from my school to the Valley, I'll catch a glimpse of a lone figure wandering the streets, a tall, thin figure with one shoe. One very expensive-looking shoe.

And I wonder . . .

The End

PRIDE

Adorning the vast front lawn in front of Mark Frost Academy was a statue of a quarterback. He is carved of sandstone, his arm forever reaching back from his shoulder in a throwing motion, the stone football grasped lightly in his large, sure hand. His eyes are searching, his curls poking out from under his helmet, as hypnotic as Medusa's pets—his entire visage so human and so fluid that you find yourself looking ahead for that perfect spiral.

(Yeah, I know my first-and-ten from my Hail Mary. My mom and I have watched NFL football since I wore

Raiders diaper covers. Try being a 49ers fan in my neighborhood—won't happen, my friend. And if it did, it—and you—wouldn't last.)

The first day I attended Mark Frost Academy, there was a press conference on that same lawn. Camera crews from all the major networks (CBS, NBC, ABC, TMZ) were there. The entire school was out in force—from the little ones in their uniforms to the older kids in their . . . shorter uniforms. My mother, the inestimable Yelena Maria Gonzales, had dropped me off in her Toyota Camry before heading off to the hospital, and as I made my way up the long cobblestone walkway, I knew I was screwed. My skirt was regulation length, just past the tips of my fingers. The wealthy girls with their shiny hair and platinum watches didn't pay attention to skirt regulations.

Rich girl eyes bore holes in me through oversize sunglasses, coldly assessing my newbie adherence to the rules. Despite my pride and my natural reluctance to thigh flashing, I pulled up at my waistband.

Not enough to be a Kardashian, but it was a symbolic gesture.

I glanced around the crowd, trying to be as incognito as possible (which wasn't easy—I didn't see any brown faces, except for the security guards; I could always count on the security guards). I saw a boy who looked safe. He was wearing glasses, and when he opened his mouth to breathe (*be still my heart!*), I could see a mouth full of metal. All he needed was a squeaky voice and he would score the nerd trifecta.

"What's going on?" I asked him.

"You didn't get the e-mail?" Score! His voice could shatter glass. I smiled despite my nervousness. "Connor Superbiae's statue is being unveiled this morning." He adjusted his glasses.

"Oh, that's cool," I said. "Who's Connor Superbiae [pronounced "Super-BEE-YAY"]?" I figured he was a big-shot donor.

The boy looked at me as if his mom told him he couldn't go to Comic-Con this year. "Is that a joke?" he squeaked. His breath smelled like eggs.

"No?" I wasn't sure. I'm not a natural joke-teller, but I like to think that I have a sense of humor.

"Connor Superbiae is a National Merit Scholar." The boy's face turned red and he sputtered, as though I'd insulted his family dog. "But that's not all—oh, no. Not only does he have more hits on YouTube for his band, Connor and the Superbiaes, than Nicki Minaj and David Guetta combined, more followers for @TheConnor-Superbiae on Instagram (and the only eighteen-pack captured on record in X Pro II) than Madonna and Jessica Alba, but at the tender age of fifteen and three quarters (as of today), he is already the greatest high school athlete to ever li—"

Mr. Trifecta was cut off as a giant roar went up in the crowd. I felt like I was caught in a human tsunami. News crews burst to life as cameramen hustled past the pulsating throng. All around me, girls screamed and boys wept. I saw a gray-haired woman in a long skirt burst into tears. I watched a bearded man wearing a straw hat wipe his eyes with a handkerchief, then wave it frantically in the air. I couldn't see what was happening up onstage, but I'd already lost Indignant Nerd Boy, who held his iPhone above the melee to record the event a thousand bobbing, weaving heads away. I was reminded of soccer games in my mother's native and beloved Mexico, where spectators were crushed and asphyxiated as fans rushed the stadium. I feared I was going down in a sea of short uniforms, AmEx Black cards, and pimple cream. A microphone whistled sharply. A voice pierced the pandemonium.

"What's up?" the voice asked.

More screaming. The gray-haired woman fainted. The bearded man passed out right after her, onto a group of kindergartners. People were rushing the stage like cockroaches fleeing a flashlight's beam. I stood my ground and prayed.

Would this be my end? Who would save a scholarship student? We few were merely the faces holding up the totem pole.

Sorry, no lifeboats for you, chica.

"Okay, okay. Everyone just calm down. I'm only a normal kid, right?"

More screaming.

"Okay, I'm kidding, obviously. My name is . . . Connor Superbiae."

I caught a fleeting glimpse of a gleaming figure at

the podium, standing in front of what appeared to be a sculpture covered in silver cloth. Upon hearing his name, the crowd went wild again and I lost sight of him.

Bieber Fever had nothing on the Connor Virus.

"This is so cool, to be honored with my own statue. I've worked my whole life for this." (He was, er, fifteen?) "I want to thank my sponsors, Nike, vitaminwater, and Red Bull."

I wasn't even allowed to drink Red Bull.

"His own statue?" I repeated to myself, though I couldn't hear the sound of my own voice. I glanced around in disbelief. Every single person was stuck on his every single word. Some held their hands together, as if in prayer. If he told us to run across traffic on the 405 at rush hour, there'd be no one left on campus.

Not me, honey. *I like me some me* is what I say.

"Impregnate me, Connor Superbiae! I want your babies!" screamed a girl running past holding a poster with Connor's giant face plastered across it. Security pulled her off to the side as she begged to bear his children.

We never had anything like this at my last school. I started missing normalcy: the sounds of gunshots, the occasional stabbing.

"Ha ha. Okay. You're going to have to ask Taylor Swift about that one," Connor said. "We met once, she's a nice girl, that's it! I have no idea what that song was about! Oh, and, speaking of rumors, I'm sure you've heard them on ESPN and Fox, NBC and CNN—and Bravo and the Food Network. I just want to announce that I definitely am not signing with the NFL before I graduate high school. I mean, I would never miss senior prom!" (More SCREAMS.) "And that goes for the NBA, too, guys! God bless you all, and I'll see you at the game this Friday. Go Mark Frost Academy-slash-Wild Pockets Banking, Ltd.-slash-Sony Badgers!"

"Take me to the prom, Connor!" a woman who appeared to be a mother screamed. "I'll wait for you!" She tore away from her identical, screaming daughter and ran up onstage in white jeans and studded heels. A security guard picked her up like lint and carried her off as she spun in his arms, clawing to get at Connor.

The crowd separated the slightest bit, and at that moment I was able to feast my eyes upon the myth, the legend, the . . . boy? Connor was blowing a kiss in the air, then "shooting" it with his index finger.

The kid was corny. He was ridiculous.

He was magnificent.

"That's his signature!" someone screamed. "Superbiae me!"

"No, me!"

"ME!"

A girl toppled backward onto me. I dropped my book bag and caught her and watched her eyes flutter in her head. "Superbiae me . . ." she mumbled. I fanned her face and yelled out for help as the crowd grudgingly started to disperse.

At least she was still breathing when the nurse showed up.

My first day. I wasn't bargaining on having a girl almost die in my arms.

And I never would have bargained for Connor Superbiae.

I have to admit, I think I, Perry Gonzales, am good at a lot of things: science, math, history, soccer, reading people's emotions, playing the clarinet, and cooking arroz con pollo. Point of fact: My small hands have never made a bad batch of arroz con pollo.

But Connor Superbiae was good at *everything*. Too good for his own good, you might say.

Think about it. What if you were always the best? I don't just mean trigonometry functions or spelling the word *Teutonic* or the simple fact that you can eat more pancakes than your three older brothers combined— I mean, EVERYTHING.

Especially sports. Any sport. Name it. Basketball, baseball, lacrosse, soccer, tennis, paddle tennis, cricket, handball, both American and Canadian football, volleyball, hockey, golf . . . and that sport with the birdie.

Ah, yes. *Badminton*.

There's a Connor Superbiae at every school, even

yours. Our Connor was tall and strapping. *Strapping* means, like, he's hot. Even I, who am made of titanium and granite and centuries of bloody warfare (are you familiar with the Mayans?), even I could see that. He was destroy-your-life hot. Girls had been sent to Connor Superbiae Rehab—there were Connor Anonymous meetings—at Promises Malibu; they offered special mother-daughter rates.

I avoided him at all costs.

Connor brushed his dark curls from his eyes when he was fast-breaking on the wood, throwing a touchdown pass, or just languidly stretching out at his desk during a math test. His curls had their own Twitter account (@RealConnorsCurlz). Their own Facebook fanpage. I saw teachers sink into a waking coma when he strode into a room with those long legs of his (that I didn't notice at all). Mrs. Swann, our seventy-year-old English teacher, forgot what she was saying in the middle of a sentence when Connor raised his hand. She stuttered, stammered . . . even giggled. Sometimes I watched her staring at him when he wasn't looking.

I know he sometimes asked her questions just to see her reaction.

Poor Mr. Rottmayer, our science teacher. He wore a signed jersey from Connor every Friday for Connor's games, and I know for a fact he sometimes did Connor's homework for him. I bet he would have taken the SAT for Connor if he'd asked. I've heard his marriage broke up because of his obsession with Connor. He told his wife he didn't have enough room in his life for both of them.

No. *Seriously.*

Connor wasn't even sixteen, but he drove his own silver BMW convertible with custom rims to school (a gift from Dr. Dre—did I tell you Connor rapped? He was signed by Jimmy Iovine, and he was in a beef with Eminem, who was said to be jealous). Everyone at school looked the other way. After all, Connor was the epitome of the Mark Frost Academy student. He was our apex.

There was a joke around the school: "What's the difference between Connor Superbiae and God?"

The answer?

"Is that a joke?"

Or: "Connor Superbiae says, 'Oh my God!' God says, 'Oh my Connor!'"

Connor was beyond the best athlete in our school; like Trifecta told me, he was also an honors student—a scholar-athlete, if you will. He had never received an A-minus in his life. (Well, there is the rumor of that one time in kindergarten when he received a check-plus but not a check-plus-plus, but that teacher was "encouraged to take a break" [fired] and hasn't been heard from since.)

Connor was a phenomenon—and he knew it.

Did you know Nike sponsored his shoes? The Le-Superbiaes? His dad, Connor Senior, a former Yale quarterback who attended med and law school simultaneously, brokered the deal. Adidas sued, claiming they already had the blueprints for the Connor 360s, but the matter was settled outside of court.

TMZ once reported that Connor was created in a test tube—that his father had literally created Connor's DNA before he was even a zygote to include the best traits of both his mother and father. I looked this up, of course—but the post had already been taken down.

The bottom line is that I didn't like Connor Superbiae. At all.

But I will say this: Connor Superbiae made Justin Bieber look like a girl.

Oh, wait.

<hr/>

I had a problem.

A problem I wouldn't wish on my worst enemy.

Connor Superbiae wanted me to tutor him. Do you understand what this meant? It was a life moment, something Oprah would document on her show. I didn't even like to look at him, much less have to sit next to him and possibly accidentally touch his perfect elbow.

So, you're asking yourself, why would *the* Connor Superbiae need me, lowly (albeit academically accomplished and all-around great girl) Perry Gonzales, to tutor him?

I shared one class with Connor—Honors Math. I held a 99.2 average.

Connor held a 99.1 average.

And it was driving him absolutely bat-shit CRAZY.

Apparently, he told his parents about this particular unlivable humiliation and requested (vigorously, so I heard) that I tutor him so he could find out what my secret is (I have none, I just study, and I've always had a comfortable relationship with numbers) and beat me. Connor has never come in second to anyone, at any time, anywhere, in any endeavor (and that's enough with the *anys*), and certainly is not going to start with my short brown self.

This is what he said to me after math class.

"Hey."

I didn't turn around. He couldn't be talking to me. I've only seen him have conversations with tall blond Viking-type people.

"Hey," he repeated. His voice sounded like vanilla cream cheese icing slathered over a hunk of carrot cake. I closed my eyes.

"Hey, Perry."

OMG. (First and last time I use that annoying abbreviation.) My hand went to my heart. Connor Superbiae was saying my name. I berated myself for being so obvious. After all, who cares what Connor Superbiae thi—

"Me?" I squealed, and felt my face burn.

"Yeah. You're Perry. Unless that's changed."

It's like the world was standing still. I heard silly boyband music and saw butterflies coming out of his ringlets. I wanted to chew on those ringlets. He stood about a foot taller than me. I had to look straight up his hairless nostrils. I wish I could say it was unpleasant.

I wish I could say I couldn't stand there forever, forsaking my past, present, and future, staring up his hairless nostrils.

I couldn't say that.

"I am," I managed. "Me. Perry."

"I want you," was what I heard.

I didn't hear, ". . . to tutor me."

"Excuse me?" Why was I hearing wedding bells? What was WRONG WITH ME?

"What's your number?"

I became paralyzed, still as that lifelike statue out on the front lawn of Mark Frost Academy. Connor Superbiae was asking for my number.

This was a game changer. College? Education? Who needed that? Suddenly, I wanted Connor's babies. I wanted his dogs. I wanted to drive his SUV with the license plate *CSHEARTPG* on it.

Connor Superbiae JUST ASKED ME FOR MY NUMBER. Do you understand?

"For my mom. She'll call you later."

How loud was the sound of a dream balloon popping?

I couldn't remember my phone number, of course—so goes my comfortable relationship with numbers—so I opened my flip phone, which suddenly seemed poor and flimsy and I was hating on my entire dismal life and bitterly ashamed of not being an app whore. Could he tell I couldn't Shazam?

But Connor didn't blink. He texted me right there and then. Trust me when I say the entire school was looking over his shoulder.

And then he turned and strolled away, taking the crowd with him. I swear Connor's feet never seemed to touch the ground.

My mother could tell something was up when we sat down to our nightly meal. It was dark outside, and the chatter and noise from the neighborhood children and families and dogs had died down. Sometimes we ate dinner at six o'clock, sometimes nine or ten or later, depending on her shift.

"*Mija*, you are humming," she said as I put my hands together in grace.

"I'm happy, Mama," I said, "that's all. I'm just in a good mood, you know?"

I told myself to shut up. I was too chatty. I didn't want to tell her about Connor. I didn't even know why I didn't want to tell her. It's like I was holding the Hope Diamond inside the palm of my hand, but if I exposed it, it would be revealed as mere dust.

Ya know what I mean?

"*Bueno.* That is a good thing. But I never hear you hum about grades. Or soccer practice. Or a sunny day . . ."

She had me.

"So, *mija*, what makes you hum?"

Sometimes, my mother was as annoying as the Mark Frost moms, but in a different way. I mean, she never wore anything inappropriate, like skorts with heels. She would never dream of piercing her belly button. She didn't consider yoga a job. She didn't have boobs that looked like shoulder pads. And forget injections in her lips (which she wouldn't need anyway—my mother was graced with a full mouth). She didn't even color her hair.

All that distracted other moms from Life (with a capital *L*) was missing from hers. Yelena Maria Gonzales could see, smell, and feel Truth (with a capital *T*) immediately; her senses had never been dulled by fears of aging, or wealth, or fashion, or diet, or where she sat at a dinner party. Possessions meant nothing to her.

My mom was the Buddha.

And today, having a Buddha mom sucked heavily.

"A boy. I mean. Not just any boy."

Yelena Maria Gonzales gave me a small smile. "I understand. How wonderful."

"Do you really think so?"

"Love is a wonderful feeling."

"Mama, he's the most amazing human being I've ever met—or even read about."

My mother knew I had read the most books of any student in elementary school, and many of them had been biographies. So this was saying something. If my mother was worried, she was smart enough not to show it.

My Pandora's box of a mouth was opened—I could not stop talking about Connor.

My mother listened. And listened. And listened. She listened through chili con queso, through scoops of vanilla ice cream drizzled with honey, and through the moment she put her feet up to watch *The Good Wife*.

She just loves Julianna Margulies's eyebrows.

At the end of my endless, intermission-free soliloquy, my mother simply asked me when I planned on tutoring Connor. I had a busy schedule—soccer practice, band practice, and clients who needed much more help than Connor.

"*Mija,*" she said, "remember your responsibilities. What happens if I don't show up for my patients because

I got a better offer? A better offer is many times just a pretty illusion."

I met Connor's mother at the Superbiae home, which has its own name, Mount Superbiae, conveniently located down the hill from Mark Frost Academy.

I've seen immense grandness in my travels—after all, my clients tend to be the wealthiest, most powerful (most anxious—and most medicated) of the land. These parents are the top .001 percent of that (in)famous 1 percent—and God forbid they don't show exactly how top .001 percent they are, so they can show the lowly .999 percent who's boss. Their driveways keep getting longer—sometimes it takes ten minutes to lug my butt from the gate to the house with a giant stuffed backpack on my back—the houses bigger, the cars shinier, the children more screwed up. The kids are like pieces in a collection that become less rarified (as opposed to more) as they age. Those cute little babies in their Bonpoint onesies become surly, pimply, billowy adolescents, objects to be ignored or, you know, sent to Utah for six weeks of "relaxation."

Connor's "home" surpassed them all. Louis XIV would have considered Versailles a miserable tear-down after walking through the Superbiae palace.

They had a ballroom, a bowling alley, a gift-wrapping room, seven trophy rooms (which were filled to the brim with various dangerous-looking metal objects), a movie theater, a music room (Connor's a classically trained pianist), an elevator, a yoga room, a gym, a "sponsor" room (which held all of Connor's gear), an indoor tennis court (and an outdoor one), a riding ring, a hot pool and a cold pool, countless bathrooms (also filled with trophies and awards), and God-knows-how-many bedrooms.

Despite the grand scale of her home, Mrs. Superbiae was more down-to-earth than any mother I'd met at Mark Frost Academy (besides my own, of course). She was pleasantly average, wore average clothes, average jewelry, and had average frizzy, graying hair. There was nothing that screamed "I live in that ridiculous palace on the hill."

Constance Superbiae seemed eager to talk. She'd been an artist in college, where she'd met Mr. Superbiae. She showed me an album with old photographs of her with a grinning young man—now her husband. She'd been a natural beauty, tall, with a halo of spirals adorning her head, a large, welcoming smile, shimmery skin the color of hot cocoa. She sighed as she ran her hand over the old photographs.

Mrs. Superbiae was now an accomplished photographer, although she didn't brag. She showed me her darkroom. I was impressed by her pictures—mostly real-life studies of children all over the world.

"These are so beautiful," I said. I was mesmerized by the face of a small child with huge dark eyes and dirt on her tiny brown face. Maybe because I could see myself in that little face.

Mrs. Superbiae's eyes lit up. "Thank you, Perry. That's so sweet of you."

"I mean it. I never say what I don't mean. I don't like to waste time."

She smiled. "Perry, I know you don't have time in your schedule for Connor, but he's so insistent."

"He doesn't need me to tutor him," I said, though it pained me. "I'd be taking your money for no reason. It's ridiculous."

"I know." She sighed. "But Connor and his father . . . they're very . . . Well, they like to win . . . They're not like me, or my other children."

I was surprised. I'd thought Connor was an only child. "You have other kids? I didn't know Connor has siblings."

"Oh, yes," she said. "We have three daughters— they're all in college or working. One just got married. Connor's our youngest. I was quite old when we had him, actually. I was in bed for about eight months of the pregnancy." She patted her belly. "That's when I really started to gain weight."

"You're perfect," I blurted out. I meant it. Constance Superbiae was a breath of fresh air. I wish my mom could have met her; in another life, they would have been friends. My mom, the estimable Yelena Maria Gonzales, had never connected with the Mom World of Mark Frost Academy. The moms were like vampires who never aged but somehow managed to look dead.

GIGI LEVANGIE

From behind, you couldn't tell the daughters from the moms. Sometimes from the front, as well—as though the vampire mothers were sucking the pretty out of their girls, rather than the other way around.

"Oh, no. I'm quite fat. But thank you," Mrs. Super-biae insisted. "See, Connor's father, Connor Senior, always wanted a son. Someone like him. Connor Senior was quite the athlete himself. He was the quarterback at Yale and captain of the tennis and lacrosse teams. So you can imagine."

"Oh, that makes sense," I said. In my head, the pieces of the puzzle were starting to find one another.

"Senior still does triathlons. He's number one in the country in his age group for the Ironman."

"Impressive." I got the feeling that Mrs. Superbiae didn't have a lot of people she could talk to, here in her house on the hill. I glanced at a clock on the wall. My next client was coming up soon. I had never been late to a client.

"I've tried to keep up," she said. "Senior even built me my own gym on the property. I prefer long, peaceful walks outside . . ."

Her thoughts seemed to drift off like sailboats on a lake. Suddenly, I heard a loud noise. My heart jumped—after all, my simple job was becoming more and more treacherous. I never knew what danger lurked around the corner.

Mrs. Superbiae sighed. "Senior's home," was all she said.

"Connie!" I heard a *clang clang clang* of heavy footsteps, metal on marble. "Connie, I'm home—another great day at the office!"

An orange man with bright white teeth bounded into the room. He was wearing one of those biking outfits you see grown men bounce around in at coffee shops in fancy neighborhoods. Lycra shorts, a cap, tight tank top, metal cleats—everything splashed in colorful, bold advertising.

It was as though an aging, neon Lance Armstrong was paying us a visit.

"Plus, I beat my own record today chugging up that hill! I made it in 28.292 seconds. My VO_2 levels were out of this world, resting heart rate one minute after was forty-nine . . ."

As he continued to stat us to death (the numbers made no sense to me—I felt betrayed), I tried to figure out what Mr. Superbiae reminded me of; finally, it came to me.

Turkey jerky.

"Connie, come on, let's take a run."

"No, thank you, sweetheart."

"It wouldn't hurt you, you know." He glowered, then suddenly noticed I was standing there. He sized me up. "Who are you?"

"Perry Gonzales is my name. Nice to meet you, Mr. Superbiae."

I held out my hand, and he grasped it in a handshake that felt like a garlic press. He released my throbbing hand.

"Perry's here to talk about tutoring Connor in Honors Math."

"Wait, what? You're the girl who's beating my Connor?"

I wasn't sure what to say. "Yes, but only by a tiny fraction—"

"There's winning and there's losing, Perry. Come on now, you know that." He bent down and looked closely at me. His face was made of striated muscle fiber. He reminded me of the pictures of medical cadavers I'd seen in my science textbook. He bore no resemblance to the grinning, carefree Yalie in those old photographs. But, then, neither did Mrs. Superbiae. Something had gone horribly, terribly, inexorably wrong on the yellow brick road from Yale to Mount Superbiae.

Mr. Superbiae stared at me. "I assume you believe in the phrase 'It's not cheating if you're winning'?"

Mrs. Superbiae gasped. "Connor Senior!"

My eyes widened. "Are you saying I'm cheating?" I barely got the question out. Insult my height, my ethnicity, my silly backpack stickers—but do NOT insult my integrity. I am, after all, the daughter of Yelena Maria Gonzales. I have a lot to live up to.

"It's just unusual, that's all. I mean, you're a girl. And you're . . ."

"Senior," Mrs. Superbiae interrupted in a soft voice, "Perry tutors half of Mark Frost Academy."

"Connor's a winner, Perry. He's never come in second in his life. He isn't going to start with Honors Math." He spit out the words as though they had stung him on the tongue. Suddenly, I imagined him with a mouthful of bees—and it didn't displease me.

Just a note to clarify, Admissions Committee. I, Perry Gonzales, have never cheated. It's not that I haven't been tempted. I saw all the cheating that went on at the academy—copies of tests hacked from teachers' computers and sold for a hefty profit, bits of paper folded more than an origami swan, entire reports plagiarized from Internet sites . . . Poor kids wrote answers on their arms or legs or the palms of their hands or copied off their friends; rich kids used calculators with advanced algorithms they'd paid a graduate Cal Tech student to devise. Sometimes they'd bribe the professor with a trip to the Bahamas. When that didn't work, their indignant parents berated the administrators until the teacher was forced to "fix" their child's grade.

The newer, idealistic teachers would start off sticking to their guns and end up soaking up the sun on a distant beach.

I turned to Mrs. Superbiae. Suddenly, I felt crushing pity for her—this castle on the hill was an elaborate, golden prison, with Mr. Turkey Jerky as the warden.

"Mrs. Superbiae, it was nice meeting you. Take care. I can find my way out." Even though I was not quite sure that I could, in fact, find my way out of this place—I should have left crumbs behind.

I pointedly did not say good-bye to Mr. Superbiae. I was afraid that what would come out of my mouth wouldn't be an apology, but a string of colorful Spanish swear words.

No one can string together invectives like an angry Latina.

I would never be sitting next to Connor, helping him with his math and secretly breathing in his scent and perhaps collecting any eyelash that strayed from his big brown eyes for my journal.

But now I was bound and determined to grind his face in my .01 percent. This ethical little Latina was hot.

<hr />

"*Mija*," my mother told me that night as I got her foot bath ready—she likes the water almost to the boiling point, with two cups of Epsom salt poured in. I'm not too proud to say I had shed a few angry tears on that bus ride back to North Hollywood. "That's just your pride talking. Pride leads to hubris, which leads to war. You do not want war with the Superbiae family."

I feared my mother was right, as always. But for the very first time, I didn't want to listen. I was too angry. I had dreams where I saw Mr. Superbiae mocking me with his orange skin and his white teeth, like an angry orange. So in the ensuing weeks, every time I would have a test in math, I had to check Connor's grade.

Our grades were posted in the hallway just outside our class. I am ashamed to say I would purposely wait for Connor to stroll up in his head-to-toe Nike gear and stand practically under him as he looked for his grade. I would pretend that I couldn't find mine; I'd start humming and acting nervous.

Connor would stare and stare in disbelief each time— because every Friday I was beating him. The funny thing was, my other grades were slipping because I cared so much about beating Connor's ass at Honors Math.

My pride became a monster, choking off my energy for my other classes, for my soccer team, for band, for my clients.

But I was obsessed with beating Connor. And that's all that mattered.

Until it didn't anymore.

I was called into the principal's office for the first time in my life. I'll never forget walking in and seeing my mother in her nurse's uniform, a light sweater around her shoulders. A worried look on her face.

The principal peered at me over his glasses and told me my grades were slipping.

"My math is great," I said. "My Honors Math couldn't be better."

"I'm getting calls from parents," he said. "You're not showing up at sessions. This isn't like you, Perry."

I had to beat him. I had to show Connor Superbiae.

"I'll do better," I said.

I was going to do better.

In math.

My mother went to bed without talking to me that night. I've never felt more lonely.

The championship game was that Friday. Mark Frost Academy was playing their archrival, Harvard-Westlake. Connor was already being scouted by NFL teams. He had reached a height of six feet, five inches and had a velociraptor wingspan. MLB scouts had wanted him to pitch before he was old enough to vote.

There were already questions about his presidential candidacy for 2032—both Republicans and Democrats were claiming him as their own. The president himself had called him twice: once to wish him a happy Easter and once on his fifteenth birthday.

Meanwhile, Connor hadn't said two words to me since the afternoon he insisted I call his mom to set up a tutoring session. I didn't think he even knew I existed.

But that day, when we were both looking at our test scores (I'd beaten him—again), he asked me a question.

"Perry, do you think it's not cheating if you're winning?"

I looked up at him. Way, way up at him. He'd grown about six inches since our last conversation. I'd grown . . . never mind.

I was about to give him a piece of my mind when I looked in his eyes. I saw sincerity. I saw pain.

"No, Connor," I said. "And neither do you. If you're cheating, you've already lost."

He did that thing where you draw your lips together when you're thinking. I wanted to kiss them. It's a horrible feeling. You ever have that feeling? Wanting to kiss someone and knowing you can't?

"Are you okay?" I asked.

"Of course." He rubbed his arm. There were bruises inside his elbow. He noticed me glancing at them.

"It's nothing. Okay?" he said.

"Connor . . ." I don't know why I did it, or how I did it, or what I was thinking. Maybe for the first time in my life, I didn't have a thought in my head. It was like instinct took over, in all its ancient glory.

I reached up and grabbed his silky curls and brought his face down to meet mine.

And I kissed him.

And when I was done kissing him, I said words that Yelena Maria Gonzales had said to me many times when I felt pressure to do more, to say more, to be more.

"You are enough."

He looked at me. And then he ran off.

I mean, like, literally ran off.

(I've had more success with kissing since then, I'll have you know. Not *everyone* runs away after kissing me.)

You've heard of the Super Bowl? March Madness? They wish they were a Mark Frost Academy championship football game.

The new stadium, provided by Lucasfilm, was filled to overflowing. Every single student and their parents were there to see Connor Superbiae lead our MFA/BofA/Sony Badgers to our first unbroken winning streak in twenty-five years. Again, news crews were there to capture Connor's every move.

I was in the stands with the band, going through the

motions of Earth Wind & Fire's and Neil Diamond's greatest hits on my clarinet.

I had found out a little about myself. I do have emotions.

Admissions Committee, that kiss with Connor Superbiae got me twisted (in the words of my friend Cleo, who lives with her two bouncing babies in the apartment below us. She's twenty-one and she's been "twisted" over her boyfriend since she was sixteen). I felt like a woman for the first time in my life.

That's a lot of pressure for one kiss.

We were in the fourth quarter; the score was tied.

Connor's dad had been on the sidelines the entire game, on the field next to the coaches. With every denied touchdown or loss of yardage, Senior would scream and turn bright red like a tropical fruit, throw his sponsored cap on the ground, and stomp his feet. He'd yell at Connor from the sidelines, slapping the side of his head. His angry spittle sprayed the evening air like a mist.

Third down. Connor fumbled the ball and recovered. Our coach called our last time out.

Thousands in the stands held their breaths and

prayed. The stadium had become a cathedral, their god a boy with the number 10 on his back. And bruises on his arms that only I could see.

Senior rushed Connor as he hustled off the field, picked him up off the ground by his helmet, and screamed: "THE SUPERBIAES ARE NOT LOSERS!"

Plus, all kinds of things that are unprintable here—unless, Admissions Committee, you like hearing words that would make the skin on your ears peel.

Senior wasn't finished; his veins were popping out of his muscled head. His shouts could be heard throughout the stadium. The bandmaster lifted his baton to drown out the litany with a tinny rendition of "Serpentine Fire," but the stadium still echoed in Connor Superbiae's humiliation as the team, for the last time, hit the field.

<hr/>

Connor went back for a pass. A tie was unacceptable. We were going for the win. The crowd roared; the noise was deafening.

Senior's screams reverberated above the din.

While his line struggled to hold the defense at bay, Connor suddenly stopped in his tracks and stretched out his arms, our Jesus in a football uniform.

Now still as his statue, Connor tilted his head back, as though offering his body, his entire self, up to the Fates.

The crowd was stunned into silence.

The last sound I heard before I fainted was the crack of his vertebrae snapping.

When Connor was in the hospital, after he came out of his medically induced coma, he asked me how I knew to say that to him. That he was enough.

When did I get so wise?

I was born this way, I told him. It's really my mother. You'd have to know her. And then I fed him another bite of my arroz con pollo.

He told me, between bites, that he'd like that.

Connor's dad moved out a few months later. He's

awaiting trial on charges that he injected his son with illegal growth hormone and steroid-mimicking drugs to grow muscle, enhance sports performance, and get those sponsorships, yo!

Unfortunately, the drugs weren't regulated by the FDA. Their major side effect? Besides hair loss, acne, bloating, and gas?

Turns healthy bones into dust.

Connor's spine is like an old man's. His bones are punctured by tiny pinpricks. He's lucky he's still alive.

After the divorce, Connor's mom sold their huge estate to Eddie Murphy, who's planning on tearing it down and building something bigger. She and Connor moved to a smaller, cozier home down the hill from the estate but still close to Mark Frost. One of his sisters transferred to UCLA and moved back home. Sometimes, I go over after school and tutor Connor in math—even though we all know he doesn't need it.

Sometimes, we sneak kisses. Because that's something we both need.

And he doesn't run off anymore. And no, it's not just because he's paralyzed from the waist down.

Smart asses.

His mother walks Connor to and from school every day, pushing his wheelchair along the side of the road. The walking has helped her regain her shape.

One morning, I waved to them from my mother's car, then glanced back at my mom. "He's much smaller than he was, huh, Mama?"

"Oh, no, *mija*. Look at him. Really look. His pride made him small. He is so much bigger now."

I looked in the rearview mirror.

My mother, as usual, was right.

To other people, Connor is tragic. To me, he is heroic.

You know how I know I love him?

He beat me in math by one point the other day. And I didn't even care.

Meanwhile, Connor's statue has been taken down.

For repairs, they say.

The End

#coda7

Alison Furia

Bennington College Admissions Committee

1 College Drive

Bennington, VT 05201

Dear Ms. Furia and Admissions Committee members,

Thank you for your letter dated May 2, 20—. It
was gratifying to learn that my somewhat unorthodox
approach wasn't wasted. And yes, as you said in your
letter, I do have at least three years before I actually have
to apply, but as you can see, these stories presented
themselves to me, and I'm only human (mostly, as it turns

out) and I couldn't wait three years to expose them. Sometimes Christmas comes early, right? Sometimes life gives you improperly wrapped, complicated gifts that you have to open. Sometimes those gifts don't seem like gifts at all, but like punishments that will only get worse if you ignore them.

So you open the gift.

And what you get is what you get (as my soccer coach would say).

Which brings me to the Seven Deadlies.

What I've discovered about myself since I sent off my application, Ms. Furia, will blow your mind. No, truly— it's beyond comprehension. You won't believe it. You may even think I'm crazy, or that I'm one of those creepers posing as a fourteen-year-old girl to get attention that I don't get from my husband or wife. That maybe I have five kids at home or I just got laid off from my job and I came up with this idea at Starbucks, standing in line waiting for my nonfat latte.

No. Not this time.

But first, let me get back to our sins.

You know, the Seven Deadlies, which I wrote of like

they're, I don't know, fantasy, like vampires and zombies and smokin' hot werewolves . . . no, the Seven are us, they're the story of mankind. The Seven are our history, as old as the oldest tree, the first wave. I don't look at people as people anymore. I look at them as sins. "What is your name?" is no longer my question. I never ask "What is your job? What do you do during the day?"

Forget the labels—student, teacher, musician, grocer. That's too easy.

I look at someone and wonder, What is your sin?

What about you, Ms. Furia? Be honest. Is it pride? Gluttony? Sloth? (I doubt it's sloth—you're the head of the Admissions Committee, and you wrote me back within three weeks of receiving my application—but you tell me. Compensation is a strong motivation.)

Do you believe in fate, Ms. Furia? Do you believe that there's a plan for all of us, a master plan laid down by an ancient hand before even the stars were born?

Well, of course not. I mean, I doubt you're going door-to-door on weekends carrying a passel of pamphlets. I know I didn't believe.

Now, I kinda sorta do.

But first, you're probably wondering if Connor (or "Pride") and I are still an item.

The answer is no. We had a good run, Ms. Furia. We're not dating anymore—although our dating consisted of stealing sweet, soft kisses between calculus problems. I learned that the slightest brush of a hand could be as thrilling as those kisses . . . that gazing into another human being's eyes for seconds could linger a lifetime in the heart.

We're still friends. But hey, this isn't Twilight. *I have band practice, you know. We didn't last forever, but few things that beautiful last forever. We loved each other fully, but more like brother and sister, in the end, than boyfriend and girlfriend.*

He helped me through a difficult time. I helped him through a more difficult time. Life is like that. Love is like that. It picks you up and carries you on this magic carpet ride, and then suddenly you drop out of the sky into your normal life, back at your apartment, your band practice, your homework, and your clients. And all that you thought would make you the happiest girl on earth becomes . . . normal. Everyday. Pedestrian, even.

SEVEN DEADLIES

And those lips that held a thousand dreams and
endless promises, they are just lips, and they belong not to
a god, not to your personal savior, not to a hero celebrated
in stone, but a person. I'm sure this feeling happens to
everyone, even to whoever married The Rock.

My mother, the estimable Yelena Maria Gonzales, says
this is the ultimate challenge of life—not to find
happiness, but to see it.

After I sent my application off, my mother sat me down
for a talk. I knew she had become concerned over my
obsession with the Seven, how I imbued bad behavior with
biblical meaning. I had become a fanatic, spending every
spare moment (spare moments being rather spare in my
life) researching the Seven Deadlies, as I like to call them.
(I wanted to make them hashtag-friendly, give them a
catchy social media moniker.) I set up an Instagram
account where I took pictures of people, babies, dogs,
flowers, insects, anything that would fit into the
#sevendeadlies chest of drawers. I tweeted about the
#sevendeadlies (@perryseven). I gathered followers.

And more followers.

*And before you knew it, Ms. Furia, I had ten thousand
followers. And that ballooned to a hundred thousand.
Then a million. Jimmy Kimmel's people called me up to
see if I would go on the show. My mother told them it was
a ridiculous request of a fourteen-year-old, and that of
course I couldn't stay up that late, and how did they get
this number?*

*Ms. Furia, you may not know this, but I'm giving
Justin Bieber a run for his money on Twitter. And
Madonna, High Empress of the Seven Deadlies, follows
little ol' Perry Gonzales (@SevenDeadliesGurl) on
Instagram.*

*My research revealed that the Seven Deadlies preceded
biblical times. Think about that—somewhere between
dinosaurs and Baby Jesus, there were Lust, Gluttony,
Envy, and so on. Thousands and thousands of years ago,
some caveman in an animal skin was painting a rock in
his own blood after killing a lion. Pride!*

*Thousands and thousands of years after that, some
dude in a robe decided that he would show the rest of the
robed dudes that he was smarter than they were and wrote*

his feelings and observations down on paper (or whatever
passed for paper in those days—papyrus?) by candlelight.
And he attached names to these feelings, or sins.

And soon, each sin had a demon linked to it—and
each sin had its own corresponding virtue. So someone
decided—maybe someone in a fancier robe, like with gold
thread and maybe a big satin hat and ermine collar—that
gluttony should have temperance, that wrath would be
coupled with patience, pride with humility . . . You get
the drift.

Each sin had its own demon; each virtue its own
angel.

Think about this, Ms. Furia: Basically what these guys
were doing was working on their Ph.D.s in psychology.
Because, of course, we all have these sins within us.

#sevendeadlies #thehumancondition

Well, my mom put her (tiny) foot down. I mean, I'd gotten
through my first year of high school with flying colors
(not sure where that phrase came from #flyingcolors)—
but was basically drowning in a sea of hashtags
and selfies.

Yelena Maria Gonzales drew the line at selfies.

"Mija," she said, staring at me over the kitchen table.
"These selfie things. They have to stop."

"Oh, Mom. Everyone selfies. Pride is, like, the
collective sin of our generation. Pride and envy," I said,
then pursed my lips and took a picture of myself looking,
I don't know, prideful.

She grabbed my phone. My mother has never been one
to make fast moves. She's more of a slow and steady,
thoughtful-mom type. Patient, wise, accepting. But then,
she's never been up against a smartphone (yes, I broke
down and got one).

Ms. Furia, you'll have to promise me that what I
say to you, that these words, my recounting of my
conversation with my mother, will never be repeated. For
one thing, the world is counting on your utmost
discretion.

For another thing, I don't want to disappoint
my mom.

(Plus, she would kill me.)

"Mija," she said, "I should have told you something
at thirteen. At thirteen, you were old enough to hear, but

*you were starting a new school, and I didn't want you to
get distracted. You had already overcome so many
challenges—"*

"Mom? What's wrong?" *My mother had a look on her
face that I'd never seen before. She was pained. But I
gleaned a more specific emotion: guilt.*

*She rubbed my hands between hers, then reached out
and touched my face.*

"I love you so much, angelita. You know, you are mi
vida. Mi corazón."

"Of course, Mama." *I found myself starting to cry.
I'm not too proud to admit it. And by now, you know it
takes a lot for me to cry. My mother's big, sad, guilty eyes
devastated me.*

*And then, as we sat there in the stillness of the
kitchen, serenaded by the distant howls of a newborn,
she told me the story of my birth.*

*On the night of my mother's sixteenth birthday, she was
visited by a vision.*

*The vision was frightening, overwhelming to a girl
who'd grown up barefoot in the mountains, who called*

*coyotes and wolves her friends and fed wild jackrabbits
from her outstretched hands.*

The vision came to her in the blackest hour of night.

*He was an angel, the largest being she'd ever seen,
with giant flapping wings that blew her long dark hair
back from her face and revealed her nightgown under a
thin blanket. He hovered above her, making a great noise
as her baby sisters and parents slept soundly in the one-
room adobe. His wings sounded like the sails on a
phantom ship and felt like a windstorm had blown in
through an open door. Her eyes were open, but she lay
still, unable to move or cry out as her body shuddered
and quaked.*

He spoke to her.

*"Do not be afraid, Yelena Maria. You will have a baby.
She will be powerful and wise. She is the chosen one. You
will raise her far away from here. En el norte."*

*Several months later, my mother ran away from home
and gave birth to me at a Catholic hospital in San Diego,
California. She named me Perry after a nurse who held
her hand as I entered the world.*

And there, in San Diego, a few weeks later, as she

nursed her new baby, she saw my father at the oldest church in California. No, not in the pews. Not in the congregation.

My father was an oil painting.

My mother couldn't believe what she was seeing. She sat there, clutching her baby girl to her chest to keep her from crying, her eyes as wide as planets.

His name was Michael.

Like a bolt of lightning from the sky, her life, and mine, suddenly made sense to her.

My father was the guardian angel Michael. The angel of all angels.

So this is why I'm here. This is why I see things that others don't see. This is why the Seven come to me, even in my dreams.

This is what they call a "game changer" on ESPN.

For obvious reasons, Ms. Furia, I am obligated to keep this information quiet. Like they say in the first ten minutes of those action movies where the fate of the world is resting on the shoulders of, say, Will Smith or Denzel Washington, no one must know.

No one must know.

The fact that I'm the offspring of the most powerful archangel in all history doesn't change much of anything. Think about it. It doesn't make me a better clarinetist or popular or even taller. (You'd think I'd be taller, by the way. I mean, my dad looks like he's an NBA center.) If I quit school and tried to get a job, I couldn't put his name down on my résumé. It's not like I can even use nepotism to mop floors at the church.

Being the daughter of a godlike figure is not as helpful as you would think. I'd be better off being the daughter of an agent, in this town. In this town, agents are gods.

Who would believe me, anyway?

Probably not even you.

Once again, I thank you for your consideration. I hope your day is going well.

Sincerely,

Perry Gonzales

Dear Ms. Furia,

This is Perry's mother. My name is Yelena Maria Gonzales.

What I am about to say is very painful for me. A mother should never have to say what I'm about to say about her own child.

Everything my daughter, Perry Gonzales, has told you is a lie. Everything. For her, there is no soccer practice, no band, no tutoring of misfit children.

Forgive me.

Her stories are, let's say, manifestations of her elaborate imagination. These things are not real—angels, demons, devils . . . of course they are not real. Ms. Furia,

I raised my daughter in the Church, and even as a tiny

baby, she was fascinated by stories from the Bible,

enamored of the magical elements of Catholicism. She'd

ask me so many questions, Ms. Furia, even as we sat in on

services. I went every day; maybe I shouldn't have, looking

back, but I was just a teenaged girl with a baby. I had no

job, no money, God forgive me, nowhere else to go. The

Church gave me peace.

Perry was especially interested in the angels. She

would ask me where her father was, and she knew his

name was Miguel, and she would say, "Mama, my father

is Michael, the Guardian of all Guardians."

She was three, Miss Furia.

She was three, without a father. I was so young and

lost. So I didn't tell her she was mistaken. I never

corrected her. She was three and she wanted a father, Ms.

Furia. And it was just something that made her feel better,

believing that her father didn't choose to leave her, and me,

her mother, but had to. And that he loved her very much,

and even though he wasn't living with us, he was always

with us, always watching over us, keeping us safe. Making us special.

You should have heard her, Ms. Furia. Perry was very verbal—at twelve months she was already speaking two languages. And everything in her mind was as real to her as if it were the concrete she walked on, as real as the chair she sat on, the bowl she ate from.

I never told her she was wrong.

This is my sin. My greatest sin.

I thought she'd long forgotten the notion of Michael being her father. I thought this chapter was behind us.

This is not to say that my daughter is by nature a liar. By no stretch of the imagination. Because liars know, on some level, that they are lying. She does not know; she has no idea. She is convinced that these things are true. And Perry is advanced, let's say, in her storytelling skills. Her IQ has been measured—and yes, it is, as various schools and doctors have told me, off the charts.

This has not made her life easier.

She can't attend a normal school. She's never actually stepped foot inside Mark Frost Academy. I can't work.

I earned my nursing degree, but had to quit so I could stay home and raise my daughter when her "unusual behaviors" and vivid stories crawled into her life, then choked it off. Her life, and mine.

How do we live? Very carefully.

I am assuming that this correspondence between you and my daughter will be kept under the utmost confidence. And, of course, it is a given that I expect and would be very grateful to you to keep this letter completely private.

I thank you.

Yours,

Yelena Maria Gonzales

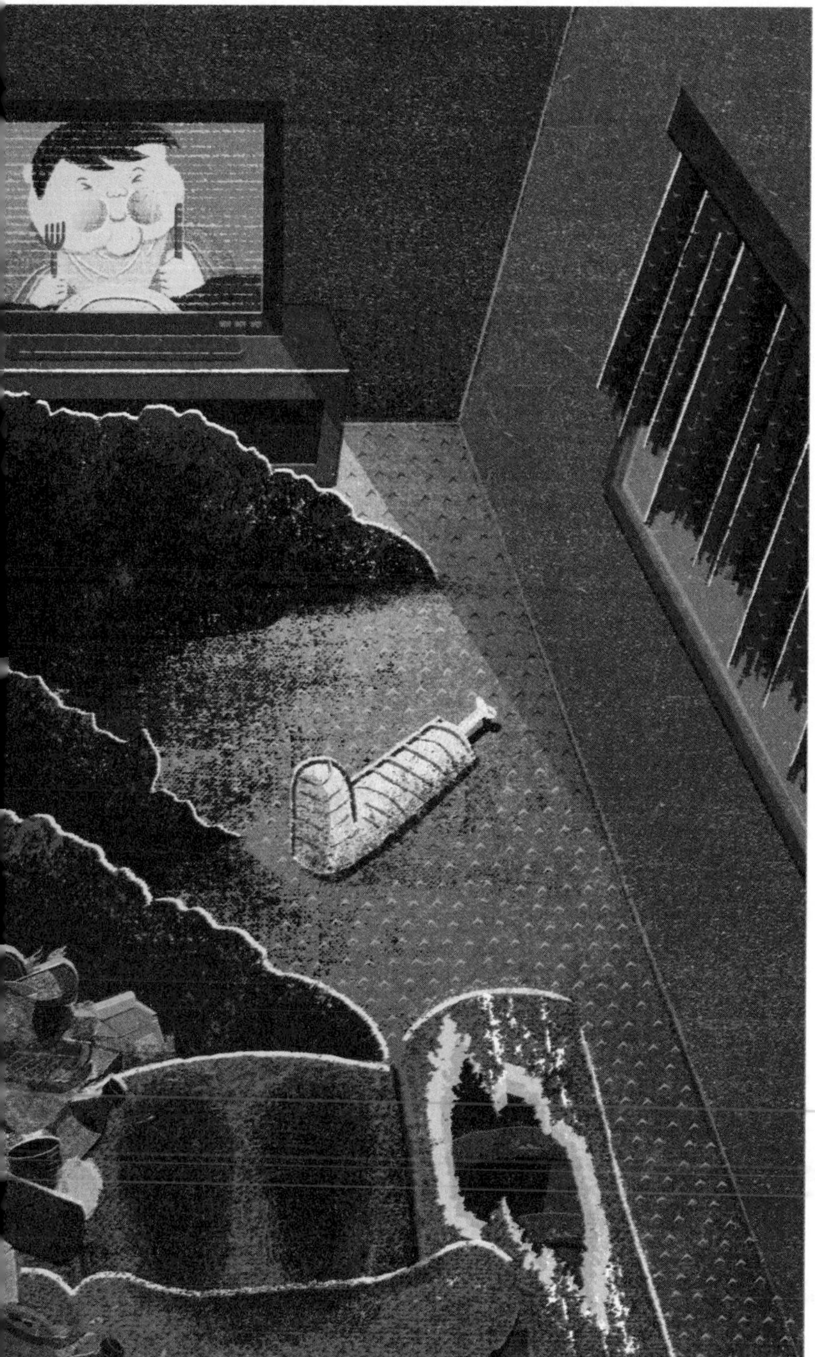